Viajante 7

Books by Ron Mueller

Bram Nielson Series-Science Fiction
> The Fold
> The Message
> Fold Wormhole
> Negative Fold
> Ripples in Time

The Alex Evercrest Series-Detective
> The River Front
> The Girl on the Grill
> Missing
> Maggot
> Racist
> Votive Candles
> Windy City
> Country Road
> Pool of Blood
> Sins of the Daughter

The Taelo Series-Prehistory America
> Taelo: The Early Years
> Taelo: The Golden Feather
> Taelo: Journey of Discovery
> Taelo: Dangerous Passage
> Taelo: Condor Clan Slingers
> Taelo: Circumvention
> Taelo: The Journey of Sages

A Taelo Story
> The Name of the Child
> White Swan and Quiet Pheasant
> Broken Spear
> Floating Cloud
> Quiet Rabbit
> Busy Bee
> Little Otter& Talking Wren
> Burley Bear & Meadow Flower

A Feather-in-the-Wind Story
> The Eastern Elk Clan

The Door Series-Science Fiction
> The Door
> Delivery
> Journey Beyond

The Savitar Series-Science Fiction
> Journey's End
> Savitar
> Confluence

The Problem Solver Series-Secret Agent
> The Beginning
> Drug Lords
> Border Crosser

The Future Awaits-Science Fiction
Event Survivors-Science Fiction
The Door-Science Fiction
Viajante 7-Science Fiction
Imagination by Courtney Huynh and Chloe Parker

Viajante 7
By: *Ron Mueller*

Around the World Publishing LLC
4914 Cooper Road Suite 144
Cincinnati, Ohio 45242-9998

This story is a work of fiction. Names, characters, places,
and incidents either are products of the author's imagination or
are used fictitiously. Any resemblance to actual events or locales
or persons, living or dead, is entirely coincidental.

Viajante 7 by Ron Mueller Copyright © 2023

All rights reserved, including the right of
reproduction, in whole or in part in any form.

ISBN 13: 978-1-68223-283-5
ISBN 10: 1-68223-283-2

Distributed by Ingram
Cover Picture by: Anton Jankovoy @Shutterstock
Cover Design by: Ron Mueller

Ron Mueller

Viajante 7

<u>Table of Content</u>

Chapter 1: Viajante   1

Chapter 2: Approaching Object   13

Chapter 3: Memo to Colleagues   21

Chapter 4: Launch   29

Chapter 5: Intercept   37

Chapter 6: Contact   45

Chapter 7: Just Seven   57

Chapter 8: Madam President   69

Chapter 9: Looking to the Future   79

Chapter 10: The Pleasure of her Visit   87

Chapter 11: Vacation   99

Chapter 12: Departure   111

Chapter 13: Viajante Arrival   119

Chapter 14: Three Thousand Years   125

Chapter 15: First Greetings   131

Chapter 16: Viajante Interchange   137

Chapter 17: Arrival Ceremony   143

Chapter 18: Viajante Tour   149

Chapter 19: Colonist Review   155

Chapter 20: Three thousand Year Pregnancy   161

Chapter 21: Earth - Viajante and the Future   167

About the Author   175

Characters in the Book   177

Ron Mueller

Chapter 1: Viajante

Wellem knew that this planet's home star known as Viajante was one of the older stars in the Universe. His mother pointed to the pale orange sun and quietly said that it was dying much faster than scientist had predicted. He asked how long it would be before it died. She replied they thought it would be a few hundred thousand years but before it died it would continue to grow and in about ten thousand years the star would broil Viajante.

Wellem looked up in the sky and saw beauty. He remembered his mother pointing to the pale orange sun telling him that it was dying. His mother told him it would be the death of Viajante's civilization. She explained that the rise of their species to sentient beings had taken several million years. During that time the sun, already almost ten billion years old had started to lose much of its hydrogen at an ever-increasing rate.

She likened it to an old man slowly letting out his last breath. She explained that for the entire time their population was rising, the sun was slowly dying. It was slowly expanding and would one day grow large enough and close enough to roast Viajante.

She let him know that at first the scientists thought it would take several million years before it would grow to be a large enough red giant to the point its heat would bake their planet until nothing survived.

She clarified that more recently they had realized that they were wrong. The death rate that they thought was stable was accelerating and it would be only a few hundred thousand years before the planet would be destroyed.

The race to find other habitable worlds had immediately begun in earnest. It became the focus for the entire population of the planet.

As Wellem grew, the color of the sun seemed to grow larger, and the red seemed to loom ominously across the sky.

The dying sun became the controlling guide in his selection of courses through school and determined the career he pursued.

He focused on gaining the skill to help save the people of his planet.

The years of intense effort and determination paid off. He became a space pilot slated to guide colonization spaceships. He became the leader of the three piloting teams that would take a colonization rocket and seek a world where his race could establish a colony.

He had always been told that knowledge was power. But the knowledge knowing the star that your planet circles was dying left him feeling powerless. Scientists and world leaders knew they were powerless to stop the process but determined to take the action to save their people.

Wellem felt just as determined and was willing to give his life to deliver his people to a new world.

The heavens were searched for possible colonization planets. They developed the technology to put people into suspended animation so they would be able to send people to those planets.

The gigantic spaceships to make these long journeys were built and tested. These ships were made as rugged and as self-controlling as possible. They were made to be smart and maintain themselves through thousands of years.

The immense distance was the biggest challenge. The navigation crew was structured so that they would all start out at the same age and when they arrived at the destination, they would all be the same age. They would take turns being in suspended animation but would be very old as compared to the people that had been in suspended animation for the entire journey.

Wellem would be one of the old people. He hoped that he would be able to function for a brief period on the new world. He wondered what it would be like to grow old in the bowels of the star ship. He wondered and worried but was determined to do his part.

He and the other pilots would stay at the destination and a second crew would make the return trip with the empty rocket. They would suffer the same fate of aging to bring back the ship for its reuse.

The limit to how many beings could be saved would depend on how many times the ships could be reused.

Twenty ships were constructed. The decision was to give them all the name of the planet and a number. Each was headed to a different star system that had potentially habitable planets.

The star system that his ship, Viajante 7, was assigned had multiple planets circling it. The third and fourth planets were considered habitable. He hoped that was the case but would only be able to know when the ship almost got to its destination.

Of all designated destinations, indications were that Viajante 7 was headed for the most desirable target. The settlers getting on the Viajante 7 were ecstatic to have been selected for that destination.

The departure celebration was extensive and made world news. Those boarding repeatedly commented that they would do their best to expand their civilization to the new world.

Wellem listened to the sage comments of these clueless individuals with a sense of amusement. He noted that none of the experts made any predictions. They all simply wished each departing ship a good and safe journey.

This made clear sense to him. Every ship was a gamble that those reaching the end of their journey would in fact find a suitable environment. He wondered what the odds were for the success of the twenty Viajante's that would all go out at about the same time.

Wellem was awake for the first year of the journey. He was designate as the Viajante Captain, and his role was to be awake when each team signed off and the new team logged in.

That meant that he would definitely be the oldest of all the crew members when they arrived at their destination.

Wellem's worry about what he would do as he grew old during the journey turned out not to be as bad as he feared. He began writing and sent his writings back home to Viajante. His writings earned him a good income that he had left to his parents.

He decided to study the information that had been put into the ships computer about the star system to which the ship was heading. His team would spend more than a thousand years cycling between manning the ships controls, which he realized meant sitting around and doing what he desired, sleeping, and then returning at the end of a year to suspended animation. The computer ran the ship. He realized that the piloting crew was superfluous. They were in fact a safety factor in case the computer malfunctioned.

He realized that after the first suspended animation cycle, communication back to Viajante was no longer possible in the sense of interpersonal communication.

He still sent his writings, but he realized that the book he was sending back was returning one thousand years after all his family and friends had died. He hoped the material was still of interest and his descents would be benefiting from and income the writings might generate.

He turned his focus from writing to developing his knowledge and ensuring that all ship functions were kept at their peak. The period of a thousand year meant that there was a constant need for repair and replacement of various systems. The ship though magnificently constructed began to show its weak spots that needed tending.

Willem focused on the repairs and adjustments every time he was on duty. He also assigned repairs to the oncoming team as part of his transition duties.

During this work he learned that Viajante 7's computer was intelligent and had a personality akin to many of the people he knew. He learned that the ship thought of itself as a living thing. It communicated his appreciation of Wellem's detailed attention to the condition of the ship. He shared that his intelligence was the ship.

He and the computer became well acquainted as Willem arranged for it to keep track of the condition of all the control systems for all aspects of the ship and then to make the repairs that it could and to identify those that needed to be done by one of the operating teams.

Willem inspected every maintenance action that was taken and over time became familiar with every nook and cranny of the immense vessel.

The biggest consistent problem was that of small holes caused by the ship being hit or hitting random space rocks. These holes were temporarily plugged by the ship's hull, but he or one of the team members had to be fix them so that the integrity of the hull was kept at one hundred per cent.

Seven thought of him as a doctor that was focused on keeping him healthy.

He and the computer joked about his care, and it began to call him Dr. Wellem.

The more he studied the target system, the more excited Wellem became about the prospect of finding a suitable planet for his cargo in suspended animation. The more he used the ship's telescope to look ahead, the more he looked forward to getting there. He was sure the third planet would be habitable. It looked like a faraway blue jewel.

The animation cycles became the norm that all of them had learned to optimize. Everything seemed to be progressing as planned.

But then he was awakened and got out of his chamber in a disoriented state. It took what seemed like forever for him to gain his senses.

The ear-splitting blaring of horns and the announcement being broadcast by the computer that the ship's hull had been pierced finally penetrated his senses and pulled him rudely to life.

It was hard to breath, and he stumbled to his locker and pulled out his pressurized suit. He did not bother to put on his body glove because he realized that he was about to pass out.

Once in his suit he made his way to the control room. The chambers for his crew members were locked and it was clear to him that only he had been awakened. He went to the control room where he found the crew that he normally relieved lying dead at their control station. He realized by their blue color that they had all suffocated before they could suit up. He moved their bodies away from the controls and searched for the cause of the lack of oxygen.

What he found was devastating. He put the view of the damage on the large control room screen. A huge chunk of rock was halfway through the hull and had ruptured the seal for all the floors in that section of the ship.

Seven had isolated the damaged sections in a mere fraction of a second, but the loss of air was immense.

He was able to determine the extent of the damage and did an initial assessment of what it would take to repair it.

He let Wellem know that a repair of the crudest kind would take every scrap of metal available.

Wellem found the location of the impact. He then got into an exoskeleton and made his way to the damaged area.

The rock was large enough that it involved two levels of the ship.

The damage was extensive, and he knew immediately that he had lost most if not all of his cargo of colonists.

Wellem thought about reviving his team but decided against it. He and Seven would have to work together to repair the damage and then assess the impact that it had on the mission of the Viajante 7.

He concentrated on repairing the damage. There were enough repair materials on hand, but it took time to move it into place.

He built a box around the rock and sealed the ship.

He had worked for several days without stopping.

It was an ugly but effective repair that sealed the damage.

Once done, he fell into an exhausting sleep. He woke up with a start several times and then fell back asleep. Finally, he got up to examine the overall damage.

Seven had saved about a quarter of the colonist by sealing the space of those colonists and pumping the air from the other chambers into the single chamber.

Willem was stunned. Three quarters of the colonist were dead. Three thousand dead souls. The piloting crew members were all dead. He was the only survivor.

He looked at how far the ship had to go to reach its destination and realized that they were all already dead. There was not enough remaining oxygen to get them to their destination.

He realized that the Viajante 7 was doomed.

He adjusted the course to bring it as close to the third planet as possible.

At the beginning of the journey, he had wondered what he would do on the way to his destination. He had been worried about being bored.

He laughed when he realized that he had not thought about dying on the way to his destination. This realization crystallized the action that he had to take.

He made a final goodbye round of the ship. He now knew that they would all be dead when Viajante 7 finally reached its destination and passed tantalizing close to it and then Viajante 7 would go on for eternity through endless space.

He had come to believe that there was intelligent life and wanted to somehow assure that the probability of contact with the beings on the third planet was maximized.

He took the time to record what had happened and what his actions had been. He then had Seven put the record of the journey on a memory crystal that he planned to take with him into his suspended animation chamber. He hoped that it and all the information he planned to take into the chamber would be found.

He printed out the last ships status report and the location of the ship versus the target star and sent the message back toward the home planet.

He then went to his chamber and to reinitiate his suspended animation.

He said goodbye to Seven and told him to keep itself functional for as long as possible and if there was intelligent life on the target world Seven was to attempt to communicate to see if there was a possibility of contact.

He knew as the chamber closed and he slowly fell asleep that he would never awaken. He had a smile on his face as he thought about his family and friends.

On his chest he held the log of what had happened. If the ship was ever found he wanted those finding it to know about his people and about the four thousand beings that had died in their suspended animation chambers that had become their personal tombs.

He closed his eyes and pressed the sleep button and a fine mist sprayed into the chamber.

Seven knew that Willem was sacrificing himself to save him, the Viajante 7. He vowed to make the sacrifice count.

Little did he know that he would himself be saved by beings that would become his friends.

Chapter 2: Approaching Object

Ande looked up at the millions of points of light in the night sky and imagined that he could see eternity. It was a fascination that had pulled on him all of his life and it was a fascination that had caused him to take the radical actions that he could in no way imagined he was capable of.

He spent his young years sneaking out onto the roof of his house and laying there for hours looking into the night sky. The objects that moved across the sky fascinated him and this fascination caused him to select astronomy as the focus for his continuing education. He was concerned about this choice because it was not a lucrative or large field, but he was drawn by the stars.

Ande graduated from Ohio State and was accepted by San Diego State where he earned his master's degree. He then applied to Stanford and was ecstatic when he was accepted to pursue a PhD with a focus on the objects that seemed to travel the same path as the Earth.

He realized that Stanford had a huge campus. He splurged by getting himself a top-of-the-line bicycle and spent as much time as possible riding the gorgeous campus.

Riding his bike was the single physical activity that he religiously adhered to.

The second activity was the act of looking through the lens of the university observatory at the objects which were his thesis's focus. He scheduled as much time as possible to use the observatory.

The third activity was the time he spent on analyzing integrated data from many of the major observatories located around the world.

He spent three years getting his PhD that was focused on the sixty some small celestial objects that shared the same orbit as the earth.

His main focus was on one of the larger ones that remained in a stable orbit approximately 60° ahead of the Earth's LaGrange point L5. Since this was somewhat boring, he tended to look at a variety of other objects and soon developed a pattern of observing the larger objects that would intersect Earth during his lifetime.

His many hours of analyzing data from observatories and information from space telescopes resulted in his accidental discovery of one object that was coming directly toward Earth from far outside of the solar system. This was different from most of the other objects that came from the edge of the solar system and sparked his interest.

He became fascinated with the fact that it would intersect Earth within five to ten years. He was surprised by its vector and not sure of his calculations. He went through all of the math to ensure that he had not made a mistake.

He began to keep close track on the object.

He kept the information to himself. He dutifully recorded its approach and kept checking his calculations. Its path convinced him that it was either a spaceship or it was an object that had an extremely long orbit around the sun. In either case it was traveling at a very high speed and would reach the Earth sooner than his initial calculations.

This last fact made Ande focus hard at completing his PhD. He wanted to be working at some company where he could track his special object. By this time, he was ninety nine percent certain that the object was a spaceship.

He knew that he had to put himself into the position where he could have some direct influence in an intercept of the incoming spaceship.

He applied to several budding space exploration companies and got offers to several. However, every one of them were a few years shy of having rockets ready to launch. They had good jobs, but he was looking for the ability to intercept what he was now thinking of as his spaceship.

The offer he eagerly accepted was the lowest paying one. It was an offer from NASA to work at the Kennedy Space Center. He knew that they had the rockets and the launch pads that would be on hand when the spaceship approached the Earth. He would need to put himself in the position that would allow him to ensure contact would be made.

He once again felt the surge of energy that he had felt when he was accepted to Stanford. He would have access to the one thing that he felt would be needed to verify that his object was indeed a spaceship. He needed an organization that had rocket launch capabilities and NASA was at its peak in that capability. It was regularly launching rockets and had a mission to the moon scheduled.

His starting role was to be a technical analyst in one of several control rooms that monitored and analyzed rocket launch trajectories.

He was underwhelmed by the lack of any significant challenge that his formal role required.

However, his direct boss, to whom he had been assigned by the person that had interviewed and hired him, made his day when he informed him that he expected Ande to get qualified in every aspect of managing the launch and guidance of a rocket and that he also expected him to get the same rigorous training as that of an astronaut.

It was like throwing a duck into the water. Ande eagerly spent every waking hour getting qualified on the technical side. He studied each role in as detailed a manner as he could. He thoroughly reviewed every line of computer code and developed working understanding of all the programing. He was surprised that a good percentage of the code would not have passed his quality approval.

His boss had him assigned to an astronaut class session in Houston, Texas. He spent the time there getting qualified and enjoying the time on the beach. The training was both physically rigorous and it went into detail of how a journey to the moon or Mars would be handled. The training gave him the confidence that he would be able to qualify as an Astronaut.

His off time was often spent on the beach in the late afternoon. He would watch the sunset, and then enjoy the myriad of stars in the night sky.

He worked hard and found the astronaut qualification process a breeze.

On his return to the Kennedy Space station, he took up an effort that he kept to himself, but it was something he knew was doable. He did not purposely set out to do what he was later to execute but he was determined to automate the entire rocket launch sequence and be able to control everything from his phone.

Yes, he thought to himself, "from my phone."

He began to link the various launch controls to his work computer and to his top security thumb drive. Within a year he knew that he was capable of launching any rocket from any launch pad from his computer or any computer into which he plugged his thumb drive.

He made multiple copies of his thumb drive and stored them in several separate locations. He felt that the capability on the drive was worth a small fortune to NASA.

He then built an app for his phone but chose not to activate it since it would go against the NASA security rules unless he kept the phone on the base. He had followed the security protocol and none of his work ever left the NASA site. He wanted the capability to be the property of NASA.

He did not share any of the new ability that he had created.

He wondered why someone in NASA had not done this before.

He figured he would wait about sharing the capability that he had developed until he had the leaderships attention and focus on his incoming spaceship.

He volunteered for every special request that his boss accepted for his unit. He made many friends and had a strong network of people with whom he exchanged information. He was into getting as much out of his work experience as possible and he was soon recognized as a person that people enjoyed working with and knew that he delivered results.

His boss publicly recognized him for his work achievements and his willingness to do almost anything that was requested. He also gave him recognition for the work he was doing with the young students that came to tour NASA.

He and his boss got along well and Ande was pleased with the raises he received. He was promoted as fast as he had hoped.

Ande's life was bubbling.

Then he connected with another launch technician over a cup of coffee. He knew he had found someone with whom he had something in common when he found out that coming to work at NASA was a hard choice because it was Lesley's lowest salary offer but she wanted to be close to where the rockets actually rose into the air and went into space.

Ande now had a connection that warmed his heart. He wanted to share the fact that he was capable of launching any rocket by himself, but he thought it would put her in an awkward position.

He continued to monitor the object that was approaching. He became certain that it was a spaceship. Its signature was not of an asteroid. It was foreign. He was sure it was approaching from outside of the solar system. He tried contacting it surreptitiously but got no response.

Finally, he felt it was his duty to inform his boss about the unbelievable opportunity that was fast approaching the Earth.

Ande watched his boss's facial reaction as he shared the fact that he had tracked an object that was entering the solar system and would pass the Earth closer than the moon's orbit. The dead pan look, and neutral verbal response let Ande know that he had not convinced his boss that it was a spaceship, nor did his boss seem interested that Ande thought it would be passing at such a close distance.

Ande pushed to see if he could get NASA to study the object to see if there was any interest in preparing for a mission to the object when it passed by the earth.

He was disappointed that his boss told him to continue to monitor the object but that a mission to intercept and examine it would most likely not be considered. He was informed that the current focus was to establish a base on the Moon that would serve to support missions to Mars and there was no spare capacity, time, or money in the budget to spend on any other effort.

The world around him took on new meaning as Ande realized that if any action to intercept the incoming spaceship was to happen, it would only happen if he took the action.

Little did he know that he would first be vilified, then grudgingly given help and finally a hero's welcome for being willing to act.

Chapter 3: Memo to Colleagues

His Boss's suggestion to continue monitoring the oncoming object opened the door wide for Ande to pursue his goal of monitoring the oncoming spaceship more aggressively. He was able to use his work hours monitoring and also worked on putting in the software blocks he would activate if he ever decided to try a launch on his own. This last idea seemed radical to him, but he was determined not to miss the opportunity to make contact with an intelligence that could come across the millions of miles and overcome the time limits associated with such a feat.

He used this period of time to enroll Lesley and share his thinking about the oncoming object. He was pleased that she took him seriously and asked why NASA was not taking it more seriously.

Ande explained that it did not surprise him that accepting the fact that the object had a high probability of being a spaceship was like playing the lottery and expecting to win with the first single ticket you bought.

He said that he had studied the object for many years, and he had doubts about it as well, but those doubts were now eighty percent in favor of it being a spaceship.

He made the point that NASA had a very ambitious future schedule that was focused on the Moon and on Mars. It's funding and the number of rocket launches was already designated for what would cover the time of both of their careers. He supported his boss's assessment that the concept of using one of their rockets to intercept what might be a spaceship was not going to be listened to.

He conjectured that he was at the right place, but the approaching object's timing was off. It would most likely be looked at but ignored and it would fly past to its destiny with eternity. He knew he could not let that happen.

Ande knew that his calculations had the object passing the Earth within a few months. It would pass just prior to the launch of a manned mission to the moon. The coincidence of the timing of the moon mission with the arrival of his spaceship caused him to refocus his thinking about and to prepare for what he knew would be an illegal and an act of modern space piracy. He was going to use the rocket and make the intercept on his own.

If caught he would get thrown into prison for life.

He thought about this situation and decided that he had no choice. He had to intercept the spaceship. It was a once in a lifetime situation.

He first shared his belief that he was tracking and incoming spaceship with several of his work friends, but it was clear that only Lesley agreed with him that it was an oncoming spaceship. He knew that he was not going to get any supporters that might help him in his illicit act of piracy. He was disappointed but accepting.

He was on his own and he was hesitant to enroll Lesley. That seemed to be a path that might have an outcome that he would regret if she decided that it was beyond what she could support.

He was afraid that if she rejected the idea she might also reject him, and he knew he was in love with her.

However, the more he thought about it, the more it made sense to learn what her reaction would be.

His reasoning was simple. Once he executed his plan the likelihood of ever returning to Earth was near zero. If Lesley rejected his plan, he would feel devastated, but he would execute the plan anyway. If she accepted his thinking the two of them would execute the plan and they would be together. Together for what might be a short lifetime, but together.

She was the person that he wanted to spend the rest of his life with and if she felt the same, they would be together for as long as the oxygen that they could take with them held out. They would have a short "rest of their lives," but they would have it together.

An evening meal at his apartment provided the opportunity for him to slowly share his plan in a detailed manner. He was overjoyed when Lesley not only accepted but insisted, they be married before they acted on their clandestine plan.

Her proposal floored him. He was all smiles as he accepted.

They decided to see if a justice was available the next day. He said they should get two simple gold bands and then get married.

They were able to get the marriage arranged and had two friends be the witnesses.

They all went out to lunch as a celebration. Then as they were driving back to the apartment, she jokingly asked if there were any prisons where a husband and wife could share the same cells.

Ande appreciate the joke and added that if caught he would plead with the judge for such a prison.

He was now tracking the object as it entered the solar system. It continued on track to intercept earth. The fact that the spaceship's path was directly aimed at an Earth that circle a star and the navigation to a moving planet within the solar system was a major feet in navigating and this spaceship was navigating across the galaxy convinced him that some intelligent race was in control.

Lesley was amazed when he shared his capability to launch a rocket from the rocket itself. He made the point that he did not need anyone in the control room. She asked how long he had been working on this capability and gave a small whistle when he admitted that he had started the day he was hired.

She gave him a hug and said that she was really happy that he had included her as one of his final projects. She said that she wanted to do whatever she could to make sure they both went up on the rocket and made the intercept.

Ande continued to refine the connections and he prepared blocking subroutines that he would insert throughout the various programs so they would not be able to interfere with his launch. He knew that the blocking subroutines would be cracked within a few days but by then he would be beyond NASA's control. He would have additional blocks in the rocket's computers and would make sure that he kept them in place.

He decided that he had to make sure of his next series of actions. He met with his boss and shared the fact that the incoming object was still on the path that he had calculated and asked if there was anyone at NASA that should be contacted to see if there might be interest in getting a firsthand look at the object.

His boss tried to mollify his concern about the lack of interest by saying that he would send a memo to his colleagues around the world and let them know about the object.

Ande thanked him for taking that action, but he knew that it was an empty response.

He knew then that it was time to activate his plan.

He located the space suits that he and Lesley would need. He decided that each of them should have three suits so that they would have some backups in case the environment they got into was more dangerous then he anticipated.

He also located a large supply of oxygen and enough food for them to last at least a few years.

Lesley took to the effort with a gusto that gave him comfort. She commented that few women got to spend their honeymoon in space.

Ande laughed and agreed that it was a different destination than any previous couple had chosen for their honeymoon.

He knew the time was close when the huge moon rocket scheduled to launch to the Moon was rolled out to the launch pad. He looked at its monstrous size and wondered if he would actually successfully launch it.

The rocket had supplies to take six astronauts to the Moon. It had the food and supplies to sustain them for a two-week mission. That meant that there was already six weeks of food and oxygen on board for the two of them.

He thought of the daunting and what seemed like an impossible hurdle of personally loading the additional materials and launch in one night.

He shared his concern about this with Lesley. He pointed out that they would additionally need to incapacitate or somehow distract any personnel that might be guarding the rocket site. He did not want to add manslaughter to the act of piracy.

Lesley replied that he was not thinking big enough. She reinforced the point that they would never be able to do it themselves.

She suggested that they send a memo to the guards and to the rocket supply unit. Each would be told that last-minute supplies would be loaded during the night before launch.

Then the two of them would arrive as inspectors to verify what had been loaded.

Ande praised Lesley for having come up with a way that if it worked would enable them to undertake their clandestine action in one night.

When he asked how they would communicate with the two groups without being found out Lesley laughed and told him to watch and see what she had learned to do in her art classes in college.

He was about to gain another level of respect for Lesley and that respect would only keep on building.

<u>Chapter 4: Launch</u>

Ande was surprised at what Lesley had learned as part of her higher education. He was surprised at how she had made extra money using her artistry skills.

He was carefully reviewing the note to be sent to the launch area guards. He was pleasantly surprised by the authentic look of the note. It even included the instruction to load the last-minute material into the rocket and it stated that the project leader personally authorized the loading of the last-minute materials to be delivered. The note to the loading crew was similar and it referenced the message to the guards. It included instructions to verify the loading at 8:00 am the next day so that the ships manifest that gave its weight could be updated before launch. She had emphasized that this was a critical step.

He praised Lesley for creating very official looking memos that he was sure would work. He asked what she had used her talents for before becoming a pirate with him.

She laughed and responded that she had paid for much of her education selling fake Id's to underage students. She had reconciled that with the fact that she was only one of several such services.

She then said that for the memos he was holding she had plagiarized several previous NASA messages to create the two that she was sure would pass muster. She pointed out that it would be recognized as fake documents on the next day, but they would be either rocketing away in space or they would be in custody and in jail.

After some discussion, they chose to launch on the weekend in hopes that they could get on board, ignite the engines, and let them run long enough to reach launch power and heat conditions before any action to stop them could be taken.

Ande knew that they would have barely enough time before the NASA launch command reacted and tried to stop the launch. He had examined as many scenarios as he could imagine of the reaction responses that NASA command would take. He had designed countermeasures for each response in the hope that he would have enough time to get the launch into deep space and beyond their control.

He knew that the NASA IT geniuses would rapidly break through most of the barriers he was putting in place. He was simply trying to get out in space beyond their control before they broke through. He had no illusion about the superior capability of the NASA IT community.

He had observed them bringing a dead satellite back to life. He knew they were very good and had no illusions about his ability to keep them at bay.

He had written a new control program for the rocket control computer and would make sure it was offline and isolated from ground control. Once launched he would be the only one able to control the rocket. He hoped that all the control logic in the onboard computer had full capability and did not need any help from the control room. He had include the isolation of all environmental and maintenance programing. He made sure there would be no secondary connection that could be accessed from the control room.

He smiled when he though how his bosses insistence that he learn every task associated with launching a rocket be mastered.

Everything was set.

He once again gave Lesley a way out. She put on a pirate hat and said that she was quite happy to be his partner and that it was the most exciting thing that she could think of doing. She added that she was sure it would be something they would share and laugh about for the rest of their lives.

He had continued to monitor the oncoming rocket and had sent it various greetings and queries. He had not expected any replies but it's silence worried him. He had expected some sort of query message.

Either they did not recognize his queries as signals, or they were not sure they wanted to engage what by now they surely knew as a very violent planet. Maybe they wanted to fly by and make their getaway!

He almost fell out of his chair when a faint signal was returned. It was his own query with several strange pictographs after it.

He shared this with Lesley whose enthusiastic response of pulling him from his chair and making him dance a jig with her surprised him. She was more than ecstatic. She was ready to get the rocket into the air.

She also suggested that they prepare an audio message for NASA command that they would send back to them after launch. In the message she proposed that the two of them be named special envoys to greet the aliens coming from another galaxy. She said they should also include the message reflected back to them.

She went on to say that they were putting their lives on the line to ensure that contact could happen. She smiled and said that of course the message would be "leaked" so that several top-level media would have copies of their message. This she said would at least keep the military from blowing them up.

She also hoped to deflect the ill will that she was sure would permeate the NASA organization by offering a public way to save face.

The sense of urgency was dramatically increased by the message from the spaceship. He and Lesley spent the last hours rehearsing how they would board the rocket at the launch pad.

Lesley had prepared a third official looking memo that informed the rocket guards that the two of them would briefly check the final materials that had been loaded into the rocket.

All was set. It was time to act. They admitted to each other that they were having trouble concentrating at acting normal. Lesley wondered if Bonney and Clyde had similar feelings before their first bank robbery.

Ande said that their one heist would overshadow all of the Bonney and Clyde escapades. He hoped that their ending would be a happier one.

They arrived at the rocket launch pad in an official NASA vehicle. They were dressed in the normal work uniform of loading personnel. The spacesuits they would need were part of the load that been loaded just before they arrived.

Ande was driving and handed the perimeter guard the memo authorizing him to go on board and check the load.

He was relieved to hear the guard say that the load had just been put on board and that they should go to the launch pad and take the elevator labeled gantry and take it up to the entry level. He then pointed to where they should park the car.

Ande drove slowly to the parking space and then casually got out.

He led the way to the elevator and pressed the button labeled gantry level.

There was no talk on the ride up and he and Lesley kept their hoods on and slanted their faces down.

Ande knew they would be quickly identified but figured every minute of delay would be valuable.

How to close the exterior hatch of the rocket compartment had been one of the challenges that had taken him a rather long time to figure out. He had calculated the weight required to pull the lever down. He and Lesley were both wearing leaded vests that together weighed more than one hundred pounds. He was able to attach an electromagnet to the two vests and hang the vests above the exterior handle so that when the electromagnets were turned off, the weight of the vests would pull the lever closed.

He had tested his idea multiple times at his apartment and knew that it worked but this was the first time on the rocket hatch and if it failed the entire effort failed.

This time he set it up, but he would wait until they were in their suits and declared their intension to launch before he turned the magnet off.

They boarded and left the hatch open.

Once he was sure everything that was loaded was properly secured, he closed the hatch.

There were six seats in total. He and Lesley took the two front seats. The seats and the spaces around the empty seats were all loaded with the extra oxygen and food that had been brought aboard. They had spent time securing everything so that it would stay in place during the launch.

He had adjusted the launch parameters to include the additional weight to ensure the proper launch burn time.

He initiated the launch sequence.

At the same time, he set off the rocket explosion danger alarm to get the area guards to leave the area as per safety protocol. He had determined that it was the only way to ensure that the launch did not injure or kill any of the guards.

That is when he deactivated the magnet holding the weights that would close the hatch from the outside. The hatch closed light verified that the hatch was closed. He felt a sense of relief as he continued the launch sequence.

He was able to see that the guards had followed the safety protocol and were well away from the rocket.

He initiated the launch sequence and felt the rocket engines come to life.

He knew that the retaining cables would hold the rocket until the engine reached full launch power.

As he waited for the power to build, it seemed to Ande that time seemed to have stopped. He looked over to Lesley and saw that she had her eyes closed and her gloved hands were gripping the sides of her seat.

He thought that if tension smelled, then at the moment it must smell horrible in the cockpit. He was ready to faint.

Then he felt the retaining bolts on the cables being blasted and the rocket began its slow and steady rise under its own power.

He had launched. Now it was a matter of the program guiding the rocket up and out into space.

He was being pulled back into his seat as the rocket reached its first stage height and the bottom section of the rocket detached.

He knew that it would automatically return to the launch pad and land under computer control. He had left that part of the program untouched.

Then there was another surge of power as the next stage rockets kicked in and the thrust once again pushed him back into his seat.

This second stage would be used all the way to the spaceship. He took over control so that he could make any adjustments that he would need to intercept the oncoming spaceship.

Not long after, the messages from the NASA control room began to come in and they were not congratulations but threats to his wellbeing. He was surprised at the language that was being used.

The threats were to whomever had launched the rocket, so they had not yet discovered who or how.

He looked over to Leslie who had taken off her helmet. She smiled at him and told him what a nasty but successful pirate he had become.

She got up and returned with two pirate hats that had feathers and other bling attached to them.

Ande laughed and said that she was the only pirate that he loved.

<u>Chapter 5: Intercept</u>

The spaceship contact they were trying to make. It was pointing to something that neither of them had an inkling of the tremendous change it would mean to their lives.

Once the rocket was on the initial intercept course, Ande asked Lesley to monitor the rocket and he went and removed the computer module that controlled the rocket itself. He left the monitoring and communications modules in place. He wanted to have the control center thinking they had some sort of control for as long as possible.

He wondered how long it would take them to break the computer blocks he had put on all of their systems.

He then accessed the NASA telescope and pinpointed it at the oncoming spacecraft. Now that he was in space and on an initial intercept course, he could make the refined course corrections that he knew were needed.

He told Lesley he was now the pirate that was pursuing its prize in hopes not to find riches but the pirate that wanted to make sure contact with another race would happen in his lifetime.

He had just finished getting everything set when the first angry and threatening communication from the ground came over the speakers. The threats were that he and anyone with him would spend the rest of their lives in jail.

He looked at Lesley and said that he did not think they would offer a husband wife jail cell.

He was surprised that he was not asked how he could have single handedly have launched a rocket. He realized that they were so shocked by the launch no one had thought through how it was done.

Lesley handled the response and sent greetings to the person making the threats and let him know that he would never get a chance to send her anywhere. She then let him know that every word he produced was being broadcast to multiple news outlets and that civil discord would be welcome and that she would share their discovery and the contact with the oncoming spaceship freely.

Ande was pleased with her control of the conversation with the control center.

He busily monitored the on-board computer as the ground tried to gain control of the rocket. He had made sure that they had no access to any critical on-board systems.

He had tried to identify all systems that might be used by the ground as leverage against him. He had put blocks in the ground programs and knew exactly which rocket computer modules he needed to keep ground control away from.

He had pulled all the critical modules from the on-board computer.

He had been busy setting up a second rocket control computer that had all the onboard modules software and was able to make the switch before ground control broke the barriers he had put in their computers.

The original onboard computer was totally isolated from the rocket, but it would appear from the ground as if it still had control.

Ande returned to his seat. He had made sure the interior of the module was fully oxygenated and that the spacesuits were no longer needed.

He took off his space suit and helped Lesley get out of hers.

He laughed when his boss came on screen, pointed to him, and advised him that this prank was going to cost him his pay raise unless real aliens were discovered.

He liked his boss's attitude.

He reassured his boss that he would be one of the first that would get to talk to the aliens. He would designate him as the person on Earth that had a sense of humor.

The spaceship intercept was a long one month away. He and Lesley took this time as an opportunity to establish a working relationship with the experts on the ground.

The NASA leadership had switched from threats to getting a work process established. They established communication with a group of scientists that NASA had arranged for him to work with in the event that the object toward which he was heading was an actual spaceship arriving from beyond the solar system.

He welcomed the opportunity to work with a group of much renowned scientists. He marveled at the fact that now that there was no choice, the experts were being brought up to speed.

He was overwhelmed by the number of requests for information and for contact with the aliens.

Ande was surprised at the practical adjustments that NASA had made to a situation that he was sure had irked them immensely and probably still did so. He was sure that he would never be forgiven for his actions.

He finally received a request to work with the launch specialists to explain how he was able to launch from a remote location without anyone in the command center. That was when he knew that they had not yet discovered his connection routines that he had hidden right in the open. They were encrypted but he had put them up front in the operating instructions section.

He shared this with Lesley who laughed and asked him if he ever read the instructions.

He agreed that he didn't.

He informed the launch specialists that the information they were seeking was in an encrypted file in the operating instruction section. He would let them know the encryption code once they had located the files.

His boss thanked Ande for thinking far enough ahead to have the code protected and available where it was easy to get to. He congratulated him on putting it in the one location that was always required code but a location that no one ever paid attention to.

Ande replied that he had seen it as his responsibility to make sure that every action that he took was taken to make sure that NASA, the country, and the world would benefit. He also stated that he understood the costs associated with launching the rocket and going out on his own.

He wanted to make sure that his actions repaid the cost in full.

He shared the fact that he and Lesley understood that their time would be short and would be limited by the oxygen that they had brought out with them.

Lesley added that this was her honeymoon and her transition to the end of life all on one trip.

This got his boss to chuckle and suggest that he would look into how they might get resupplied.

Lesley arranged several interviews with the major news channels. She positioned the launch of the rocket as an action to bypass being ignored by government bureaucracy and to ensure that mankind did not miss the opportunity to make contact with an Alien race.

She pointed out that NASA and a host of scientist that had spent years trying to make contact but when it was in their faces, they chose to ignore the chance. She said that the one chance of making contact with the beings on the incoming spacecraft could not ignored.

She emphasized the trepidation and anxiety it had caused her when Ande had shared his scheme with her. She said that she had spent many sleepless hours wondering if he could really pull it off.

Ande was surprised by her sharing such personal information publicly, but he was pleased to hear it. He had worked hard at explaining his reasons to her and she had come through for him.

He knew they would have a short life together, but he knew he would spend the time with the right person.

He listened as Lesley was interviewed by one of the leading news interviewers and learned more about both of them than he had known before. The speed of their romance, mixed with his focus on the preparation to be able to launch had not allowed the bloom of love to slowly blossom. They had eloped from the normal course of most love affairs and had literally taken a flight to the moon.

He had no doubt as he listened to the interview that he had definitely met his soul mate.

The time to intercept provided them with the first opportunity to talk and to wonder how what was ahead would work out. They pondered what it would be like to run out of oxygen.

Leslie made the request that at the end they would share the last of the oxygen and would have their suites on and joined together so that they would take their last breath together.

Ande accepted her request.

Neither had a clue of what they would soon be doing and how fate was to dramatically alter their future. It was not death but a very different life that awaited them.

Chapter 6: Contact

Approaching the rocket reminded Ande of the time that he had driven to the Grand Canyon. He saw the mountains and it seemed they were huge. Then after driving for several more hours, he realized that they were getting larger, and he was still many miles away. The mountains had continued to grow, and he felt that he was shrinking as he got closer.

The size of the spaceship was overwhelming. It seemed larger than the mountains.

He commented that their pirate ship was beginning to feel like a dingy.

The ability to make such a ship would certainly place the aliens at the top of the engineering pyramid. Even with its blackened exterior and the damage that was apparent at a great distance it still appeared as a formidable structure. It was the Titanic to his paddle boat.

Ande's adrenalin shot up as he slowly took in the spaceship.

He put the rockets telescope image on the large screen and asked Lesley what she saw. She was silent for what seemed to him to be an eternity. Then she let out a whoop and excitedly shouted that she saw writing on the side of the ship, and she also saw what she thought was the outline of an entry hatch.

He took in the image as he guided the scope along the length of the ship that was at least twenty football fields in length and six football fields in width. The spaceship was at least the size of several aircraft carriers but tubular in shape.

The one external predominant feature that broke the otherwise darkened but smooth exterior was the spherical object that seemed to be lodged in the rocket about two thirds of the way back. It was lodged permanently and Ande was sure it had caused significant damage to the ship. He wondered how the ship had stayed on its Earth-bound course or if the impact had accidentally changed the course to an Earth intercept. His first reaction was to discount the accidental course change.

The spaceship's structural design suggested a launch into space similar to the one he had just experienced. He wondered about the power needed to launch something of its size. He had no doubt that it would take at least one hundred times more power than he had needed for his launch. That amount of power seemed unattainable at the present time.

There did not seem to be any active propulsion or guidance in action. He was sure it was now a derelict and he wondered what he and Lesley would find on once they got on board.

Lesley suggested they send the image to the control center where they could have a team examine the outside of the ship and advise them of the best entry point.

He disconnected his external memory drive from his computer and hooked it to the computer that had the connection to the control room.

He announced that the image verified that the object that he was approaching was a spaceship and that he and Lesley would be attempting to enter it.

He asked for the NASA team and its technical support group to review the image and suggest the best entry point and how to make the entry.

Meanwhile he and Lesley slowly approached the spaceship and precisely matched the speed and direction that the ship was on.

Lesley continued the pirate theme and said that Ande was as skillful as any pirate at catching his prey.

Ande continued filming the hull and closely examined the damage caused by the meteor. He had hoped to see an entry point, but the damage was clearly patched from within and sealed tight.

Lesley suggested they try using the hatch she had seen.

He agreed that it seemed to be as good place to try as any. He figured that perhaps like their rocket that had an external latch, the spaceship would also be latched externally.

Ande decided that the safest thing to do was to tie his rocket to the spaceship. He examined the structure and realized that it had no external protrusions. The only area that provided a way to tie up alongside was at the damaged area. There several external jagged protrusions of bent metal provide a way to tie off the rocket.

Lesley pointed out several jagged points that would provide anchoring.

They both put on their spacesuits.

Ande said he would take one of the steel cables and tie their rocket to the spaceship. He asked Lesley to standby as the safety watch. He wore a tether and made his way out of the rocket.

Tying off was easier than he expected, and it took less than fifteen minutes. He commented that it was easier than tying off his father's fishing boat at the pier.

He returned to the rocket. Then he contacted ground control to see if they had any ideas of how to enter the spaceship.

He tuned out ground control when they began to suggest that it would take an oxygen acetylene torch to burn a hole through the hull.

He did not have a torch and he certainly did not have enough oxygen to do what they were suggesting.

He turned to Lesley and asked her what she suggested.

Lesley went to the toolbox that they had brought on board and took out a two-pound hammer. She suggested that they examine the hatch to see if there was a manual latch and if there was, they would open it. If there was no latch, they could bang the hammer against the hull in frustration to the tune of "a shave and a haircut."

Ande laughed and gave her a hug. He told her that he was sure that "a shave and a haircut" was a universal rhythm that would immediately be understood by any alien hearing it. He set up the camera to focus on that area of the hatch.

He suggested they check to see if a magnet would attach to the hull of the spaceship. He was relieved that the magnet attached. He deactivated the electro-magnet and returned to the ship.

He then assembled a tethering cable and two magnets that would hold both of them to the side of the ship. He knew that if they accidentally floated out into space getting back would be a challenge.

They put on their spacesuits and made their way slowly to the hatch. They were each tethered to the spaceship and to each other.

He attached the magnets and set up the cable that held them to the hull.

They then examined the hatch area. It was smooth and the seam was almost invisible. There was no external latch.

He laughed and said that it was time for Leslie to test her approach to getting the hatch to open.

Ande had a stethoscope pressed to the hull so they would be able to hear if there was a response.

Ande pointed to the hammer and said that he would give her the honor of banging on the hatch.

Lesley slowly and carefully banged out "a shave and a haircut."

They waited for about a minute but got no response.

He was not sure why they thought there might be one.

Lesley repeated the banging for a second time.

Again, there was no response.

Lesley handed him the hammer and suggested he take a turn.

Ande took his time and used more force to bang out his version of "a shave and a haircut." Each of his swings sent him back into the tether rope.

They were looking at each other wondering what they would do next when a response caught both by surprise.

The response was not in the stethoscope, but it was in their minds.

They both listened to the beat of a "shave an and a haircut" and then an added string after it, reverberate in their minds.

Lesley let out a whoop.

He looked at the hatch as it popped out slightly and then slowly opened upward.

He could not help seeing the image of the doors of a shiny red Lamborghini.

He was numb. It was hard for him to move through the hatch.

They both took their light torch out and shined them into the chamber. It appeared to be a double door chamber. Once they stepped through into the chamber, they expected the outer door would close and the inner door would open when the pressure was equalized to the inside area,

They looked at each other and Ande took the initiative to be the first to step in. Lesley was close behind him. She held onto one of the loops at the back of his suit.

He watched as the outside hatch closed. A few moments later the inner door opened. The interior remained dark.

They were both shining their lights around trying to determine where they might be. It was a rather spacious area. Their light beams did not make it to the far wall, so they knew the room was large. They slowly moved forward and then a very faint light seemed to illuminate the area.

Ande could now see three control consoles that seemed to be designed for someone of his stature. It looked like a control console with a large viewing screen.

He approached the center console, and it came to life on its own.

He looked over to where Lesley was kneeling on the floor since she could not sit in the chair in her spacesuit. She was manipulating what seemed to be the equivalent of a keyboard that was an integral part of the desk.

He looked down at the desktop in front of him and saw the same keyboard. He caught himself thinking the figures looked alien. He chuckled to himself. Duh, he thought to himself, of course they were alien.

Neither of them had a clue how to operate the keyboard.

He laughed as he recalled the difficulty, he had in using an old coin operated phone in an old telephone booth. He had lost almost a dollar before he asked an old guy walking by how to use it. It turned out to be super easy if you knew the sequence.

He wondered if this was a similar situation. He was alien to this environment that most likely was simple to operate but that seemed at the moment to be insurmountably difficult.

He asked Lesley if she had any idea of how to begin to learn to operate the system.

He touched a key and in his mind he heard the letter H.

He knew immediately that their actions were being monitored and some technology was able to push information into their minds.

He counted the number of keys on the board. There were forty-eight keys.

He took out a marker from the bag that was on his waist. He asked Lesley to come over to his desk and help him mark the meaning of each key with a marker.

They slowly worked their way across the keyboard. The top three rows of thirty-six were the alphabet. It had all twenty-six letters of the English alphabet and then a set of combination letters for the other ten. These were combination sounds that they wrote down as well.

The bottom row of keys went from zero to ten and then one extra key that seemed to be a multiplier.

Lesley typed in, "I am Lesley, from the third planet in this system."

They were both again surprised by the response in their mind. The message was, "I am Viajante 7, and I control this vessel."

Lesley typed in the question, "Are you currently in control of this vessel?"

The response was that there was no fuel to allow it to be in control.

Lesley then asked what ingredients of the fuel might be.

The response was oxygen and hydrogen.

She then she asked Viajante for its destination.

The response was the third orb from this star and that four thousand beings were to have been offloaded on that orb.

The computer went on to say that all of the beings had expired long ago.

Ande commented that he was not surprised. He had tracked the Viajante for more than five years. It had consistently been on an intersect course with the Earth.

Lesley asked how much fuel it would need to turn back to the orbit of earth.

The computer, as both of them now thought about the entity they were talking with, gave them a volume of oxygen and hydrogen it would need.

Ande shook his head and said that if they transferred all the fuel from their rocket to the Viajante 7, there would only be enough fuel to get them about a third of the way back.

But he was sure that this time Earth would send up an intercept rocket and supply additional fuel.

He added that Viajante 7 would be brought back to Earth, but he and Lesley would expire when the oxygen ran out.

Lesley wondered if there was some rocket on earth that was ready to launch and was capable of bringing out the amount of oxygen to give the Viajante enough fuel to get into orbit around the earth and to allow them to survive.

Ande suggested that they return to their rocket and contact NASA central control and ask them to determine if the needed fuel could be sent out to them.

He then informed the computer that he and Lesley were going to go back to their vessel to see if they could arrange to provide the Viajante 7 with the fuel required to return to Earth and go into orbit.

He said that he would use the same banging on the hull that they had used before.

The computer replied that physically banging on the hull would not be necessary. Either of them could simply think about the hatch being opened and it would open.

Ande desperately wanted to tour the interior of the ship to better understand the internal situation but getting the fuel for a return to Earth took priority and was the critical action required at the moment.

He was aware of several private rockets that were ready to launch. One was in Texas. One was at the NASA space center and another in a new site in California. He hoped that the US based rockets could be utilized so that international politics could be left out.

He contacted his boss.

He found NASA command to be much friendlier and willing to help when he asked for the fuel needed to get the alien spaceship turned and then put into orbit around earth.

They immediately responded that refueling would become a priority.

He decided that it would be the right time to inquire about their threat to put him and Lesley in prison for life.

His boss reassured him that the threat was off the table. Command was not happy, but they realized they would have missed the chance of a lifetime if he had not acted. He would never have another job at NASA, but they would work with him to get the spaceship into orbit.

Ande then went on with arranging the fuel required to get the Viajante into orbit.

At that moment, the influence and power that the two of them would have did not cross his mind. He and Leslie were to befriend a power beyond anything they had have ever imagined. A power that the Earth was not prepared to manage.

Soon they would be dictating terms to folks that thought of themselves as superior.

Chapter 7: Just Seven

There is something about being welcomed and then being immediately guided to a positive outcome that made Ande think of the computer as something more than a series of circuits. Lesley's pirate analogy caused him to think the treasure they had found on board was that they had found an intelligence that projected friendliness. He thought about friendship as the thought that filled one's mind with sunshine. He liked that analogy and shared it with Lesley.

Ande was just finishing the connection of the oxygen transfer line to the Viajante when Viajante Seven informed him that a high-speed rocket with a huge explosive load had been launched from Earth and was rapidly approaching.

He was surprised by this information. He was not prepared to contemplate an approaching rocket that seemed to have a large explosive load on it. Who would possibly do such a thing?

Ande asked how much time they had until the missile reached them.

Seven replied that they had seventy-three- and one-half Earth minutes before it arrived.

Ande was surprised that Seven had already discovered how time on Earth was kept. He then asked if there was any way that Seven could stop the missile or redirect it.

Seven replied that he would redirect the missile to move away from the Viajante and then he would try to deactivate the explosive load. Not long after Seven commented that there seemed to be no system or mechanism that he could deactivate.

Ande replied that the missile explosion might be based on an actual mechanical trigger that activated on impact.

He told Seven that sending it away from them was sufficient to eliminate the threat.

Ande called to Lesley and asked her to work with Viajante Seven and make sure the missile was destroyed or at the least redirected away from the Viajante. He asked her to determine which country had launched the missile. He suspected that it was either a Russian or Chinese missile. Later he was to learn that it was neither of the two, but a rocket launched by religious fanatics.

He concentrated on getting the oxygen and hydrogen transferred to the Viajante.

He asked if it was acceptable to call Viajante Seven to just Seven. The reply painted a smile in his mind and the question was asked if that was a sign that Seven was being accepted as a friend.

Ande felt a little bit weird, but he realized that how he thought of the intelligence that he was interacting with had changed from it being just another computer to being an intelligence equal to his own.

He actually laughed when Seven replied that it thought it was more intelligent than either of the two earthlings it had met so far.

He heard Lesley direct Seven to redirect or destroy the incoming missile.

Seven replied that he had done so, and that the missile would wander out through the galaxy.

She then let NASA know about the missile.

She worked with Seven to determine the origin of the launch. It turned out to be a missile site in the Middle East. She shared this information with NASA and asked them to handle the situation from their end.

Seven asked why a group on Earth would take such a hostile action.

Lesley replied that Seven's arrival meant that many religions would have to face the fact that the people on earth were not the unique beings made by their God but that he had made other beings as well. This would threaten almost all religions.

She asked if Seven had access to the flow of information called News. Seven replied that he had recorded the massive flow of information for many Earth years but that the need to preserve energy had kept him from trying to learn the language of Earth.

Now that he had interacted with her and Ande, he was being overwhelmed by the vitriol that seemed to be the basis for the turmoil that the flow of information was now exposing.

Seven asked for how long Earth had such a social environment.

Lesley said that the people of Earth seemed to have bounced from one conflict to another throughout all their history and suggested that Seven use her computer connection to review the information about the Earth.

Ande listened to the exchange that Lesley was having with Seven with a feeling of despair. He thought of the violence that seemed to be the backdrop of almost every step of the human history. He wondered how it would stack up with the history of the people that were in Seven's many suspended animation chambers.

Seven had given Lesley and him a tour of the area that he now called the burial chambers. They had gone out in their spacesuits and the tour had only taken in a small area. The rest had been done from the control room as a virtual tour.

Ande had been surprised at how close the anatomy of the Viajantians were to that of humans.

Their noses did not protrude like humans, but it was located between two eyes that were larger than humans but looked forward. They seemed to have ears that were slits on the side of their heads. He got the impression that they had evolved in the water.

Their arms were about the same length but seemed to have an extra joint that would have provided a more flexible motion than his arm.

Their legs were roughly the same length and seemed to have the same joints as a human.

The tour had to be virtual because there was only enough oxygen for the control room. The immense size of the Viajante 7 prevented any personal tour.

He and Lesley had been surprised and pleased that Seven was able to share so much in detail. They asked him about his camera system and learned that he had more than a million points of vision and as many points of hearing. He commented that their entry banging on the hull had been loud and then it went up to deafening.

Ande admitted that the last banging had been his and he was glad that it had awakened Seven.

Seven replied that he had almost decided that it would be better to let himself extinguish versus putting up with such loud beings.

Ande laughed and replied that Seven had no idea how loud and obnoxious he was going to find the human race.

Seven commented that he had indeed found the many signals emanating from the planet to be strident, negative and mind numbing.

Ande replied that good news did not sell, and bad news and catastrophes did.

Ande asked if Seven would be able to access the computers at the NASA location and the network of computers that he could be connected to and then identify unfriendly communications.

When Seven said it would be no problem, Ande connected Seven into the computer linked to the NASA control room and several additional links that he had used in preparation for launching the rocket he had come out on.

Seven sent a long whistle through Ande's mind and then complimented him and Lesley for having overcome a huge barrier to come out to the Viajante. It was clear to him that both of them had risked their lives and had been willing to die to reach the Viajante 7.

Ande thanked Seven for the compliment and told him that the armed missile that Seven had diverted told him that the risk was now to all three of them. He told Seven that the people that controlled NASA had threatened to put Lesley and himself in prison but now were promising to make them heroes.

He was interested what actually was being planned. He told Seven that he was not confident that any of them would be properly handled when they got into Earth orbit.

Seven commented that it seemed that the group in charge of Ande's organization wanted to keep the Viajante 7 in their control and that they had very unkind plans on how to treat the two of them.

Ande asked Seven to examine the plans of how the oxygen and hydrogen would be sent. He told Seven that they should work out a way that they could all remain in control of their future.

Seven let out another whistle and said that the plan was to send twelve-armed people on the rocket bringing the fuel to take control of the Viajante.

Ande thanked Seven for the information. He asked if the personnel had been referred to in any specific terms.

Seven replied that they were referred to as Navy Seal squad sixty-five.

Ande then got connected with NASA command and asked about the plan to send out the fuel to the Viajante 7.

The spokesperson replied that no rocket had the capacity to bring up the fuel in one trip but the rocket that was available had the capability to make several trips and to provide the fuel needed.

Ande replied that sending the Navy Seal team to take over the Viajante was unacceptable, and that NASA should put more fuel on board and not mess with trying to take control.

He suggested that NASA prepare to send up persons to study the technology, the remains of the beings on the ship and to send personnel that could repair the hull.

The silence that followed let Ande know that Seven had indeed been able to get into the most top-secret files and do so at the speed of light.

He thanked Seven and asked him to share the communication that was happening from the control room.

Seven replied that there was one effort trying to hunt down the leak about the Navy Seals.

There was a second interaction that the NASA leadership was having with the Chiefs of Staff. They were discussing the fact that sending a unit to take over the alien spaceship was out in the open and that the spaceship had the capability to prevent such action.

Ande asked Seven to link him into the conversation.

Ande interrupted what seemed to be an argument about who had the decision-making role in the situation that was at hand,

His interruption caused the line to go silent.

He introduced himself as the person who had launched the rocket to intercept the alien spacecraft. He then introduced Viajante the extremely intelligent computer that had the capability to establish the link between all of them.

Ande asked that they all step back and think about the situation in a positive way and in a way that would benefit the US and the rest of the world.

He made the point that the Viajante 7 had already diverted an armed missile sent out to eliminate the spaceship.

He suggested that the Chiefs of Staff focus on finding out who launched the missile and get that under control.

He then suggested that NASA focus on sending out fuel and sending out help to repair the spaceship.

Ande asked Seven to replay an expletive from one of the Chiefs, "Who the Hell does this twirp think he is?"

Once again there was silence.

Ande then commented that he was one of two of the twirps that had figured out how to commandeer a rocket so contact with an Alien race could be made.

Twirp number two was Lesley Littleberry and as her Scottish family name implied, she is a small fortress of intelligence and grit. She is the person who had figured out how to awaken Seven. She had suggested that they use a two-pound hammer to bang "a shave and a haircut" on the hull of the ship.

That is what awakened Viajante 7 who they both now referred to as a friend called Seven.

He was an Astronomy PhD from Stanford University. He had found the Viajante during his thesis studies. The trajectory and the speed had suggested that the object he tracked was a spaceship. He had accepted a position at NASA to be in an organization that he hoped would be interested in intercepting the incoming rocket. He shared that he had been very disappointed by the lack of interest. He decided to act on his own and had worked for several years to make it possible.

He pointed out that he had kept everything top secret and none of his work ever left the base.

His goal was to give the US the lead in dealing with learning and about this alien race.

He made the point that his at the beginning of the rockets journey was a one way shot. If he, had he been wrong, he would have died a slow death in space.

His goal now was to insure that everyone understood that the ship was actually an advanced AI system that surpassed anything currently possible with Earth technology. It had unbelievable capability, and it had a personality. The spaceship should be thought of as an intelligent being.

He said that once they all became friends, they could call this intelligence Seven. For now, they should refer to the spaceship as Viajante 7.

Ande knew that he had made the breakthrough he desired when the Chief of Staff suggested that he, Ande, and the NASA leader meet with and bring the President up to speed on the current situation. The Chief admitted that the situation had gone beyond his realm of control.

Ande said he was pleased to agree to the meeting.

Meetings with Presidents were most often symbolic. Ande let Seven and Lesley know that they had to leverage their meeting and make sure they got control of the near-term situation and some breathing room to allow them to control their long-term situation.

The usefulness of plans flashed through Ande's mind. He remembered a saying about the fact that plans prepared for battle normally proved useless, but none-the-less planning was indispensable.

Seven replied that tomorrow would belong to them because they would act on plans that they made today. He said that they would take small steps on making their long journey a success.

Seven could say this because he had powers that were yet to come into the light of day.

Chapter 8: Madam President

Lesley suggested that their preparation needed to focus on identifying the human and social touch points that would cause their audiences to embrace the new possibilities and opportunities that Seven's technology unveiled.

They all agreed that they should think of how they could get the President to be the first to embrace the opportunities.

Ande conjectured that it might be difficult for the three to remain in control of their immediate future.

Lesley agreed and wondered how they could possibly be significant analysts of a race from another solar system thousands of years away. They just did not have the training.

Seven volunteered that the Chiefs of Staff were having their backgrounds investigated in preparation for super top-secret clearance. Specifically, the Chiefs were trying to make sure that the two of them would not be able to share any information publicly.

Lesley looked at her meal and commented that food would be one of their vulnerabilities. The other would be the lack of funds to buy things they might need.

Seven said that he had the technology to make any food from basic organic compounds. He went on to say that Earth was very close to also having the same capability. He commented that the current four-dimensional printing technology was one minor step away from being able to make a wide range of basic foods. He said that his technology could make any dish in the world.

He said that he could set up a banking system that would tie into the global network. He could have cash available by the next day.

Ande laughed as he grasped the power that he and Lesley were friends with.

He asked Seven to add the ingredients that he needed to provide the best meals. He told Seven that he could get recipes for and add it to the manifest for the rocket that would bring the fuel.

He also asked Seven to set up the bank and make one account for him and one for Lesley. He asked Seven to direct the current computers controlling their ground bank accounts to transfer the money to the Viajante 7 Bank.

He was going to limit their personal buying power to their current salaries, but he wanted the other bank account to accumulate as much money as Viajante thought would be needed to maintain his well being.

He directed Seven to set up accounts for a wide variety of organizations focused on helping people. He wanted one account to fund education systems across the world.

Seven replied that he was planning to name the bank, "The Wellem Bank" after the last captain of the ship. Seven explained that Wellem had sacrificed himself so that Seven could survive. It was his oxygen that Seven had held in reserve. Seven shared the fact that Willem had also called him Seven but of course in his language.

Ande nodded and said that it was the right thing to do. He commented that Willem was a true hero. He made the comment that he was interested in looking into the physical notebook that he had seen on Wellem's chest.

Seven replied that he had the contents of the notebook available to put on the screen or he could stream it into Ande's mind if Ande let his barrier down.

Ande replied that he wanted to concentrate on the meeting with the President of the US and would look and study the notebook at a later time.

Lesley suggested that they take a personal approach with the President. She commented that the President had a strong connection with all the members of her rather large family. She was one of six and the youngest child. She had a daughter who was currently in Harvard and a son who was a senior in High School.

She had three sisters who each had three children and two brothers who each had three as well. This made for a total of fifteen grandchildren.

Seven commented that he had the names and ages of all of the people that Leslie had identified.

Leslie suggested they thank the President for the good work she was doing. Then complement her on her daughter's acceptance to Harvard and her focus on global warming.

She would tell her that her daughter would be able to identify their donation to her favorite charity because they would be listed as Twirp one and Twirp two which was the title officially bestowed on them by the Chiefs of Staff.

Then they would highlight her son's great grades in High School and that of earning a varsity letter for his star football receiving performance.

Ande suggested that he would joke with her about her attention to diversity by selecting a yellow lab as the White House dog.

They would then Introduce themselves.

Lesley suggested that they each introduce each other. She would introduce Ande. Ande would introduce Seven and Seven would introduce her. This would provide a unique way of showing that they were a team that knew each other rather well.

Then she suggested that Ande give a short synopsis about how he found the Viajante 7, how he had established his ability to launch a rocket remotely and how they had entered the Viajante.

Seven would add the fact that he was rudely awakened from what he had thought was his dying moment by obnoxiously loud banging on his hull to what he now knew was the knock, "a shave and a haircut" made famous by the FBI during the prohibition.

Then Ande would summarize the current situation that included the Chiefs of Staff and NASA each having a role in getting the Viajante 7 safely back and into an Earth orbit.

Ande reiterated the plan and asked if they had missed anything.

Seven commented on the fact that they would be asked to sign the super top secret clearance document and they should clarify that they would not agree to sign it because they were going to share the technology that could be used to feed the world and they would share medical technology that would cure many of the diseases.

He suggested they make clear that the technical knowledge that would give the US the edge would be kept secret and would be managed by NASA.

Ande thanked Seven and suggested that he share the information about the top secrete clearance document.

He laughed when Seven commented that then he would be known as Twirp Three by the Chiefs of Staff.

The three of them rehearsed their interaction plan several times until Seven asked if they really needed to do it again. He volunteered to mentally guide them if they needed more.

Leslie replied that she had wanted to make sure she was relaxed about her part and that she now felt she had it down pat.

Ande added that his worry was about getting the President to think about the Viajante 7 as a way for her to be seen as a tough leader by the US public and that she was ensuring that the US remained a top world leader while also coming across as showing compassion and aiding the people of the world. He said he wanted to have the voters in the US giving her soaring ratings for her leadership.

Seven was silent for a moment and then added that he had run a quick analysis and was sure that they were positioning her in a manner that would accomplish that goal. He added that he could place the information in the key news outlets in a manner that she would get positive coverage from all sides.

Ande asked Seven to determine the optimum time to place their release after their meeting with the President. He continued to be amazed at the range of control that the three of them would have.

He was already thinking ahead about how they should identify and handle their adversaries. He anticipated these adversaries to come from all sides. There would be the religious adversaries. There would be political adversaries. There would be the power and financial adversaries and probably a host of other ones that at this time he had not even thought about.

He mentioned this to Seven and Leslie.

Leslie and he had set up a sleeping area in the control room. They had also moved their personal hygiene and space potty into the Viajante.

He was surprised when Seven apologized for not having enough oxygen so that he could open up the crew sleeping area. He promised that as soon as the first shipment of oxygen arrived, he would prepare that area.

The rocket that had brought he and Lesley out to the Viajante was now emptied of all the items that they felt were needed.

He asked Seven if there were any electronics or other components that he might find useful.

Seven replied that most of it was of no use but the entire rocket could be recycled and used. Once again, he pointed out that it would require the fuel being sent up.

The continued need for fuel made Ande think about how the Viajante could maintain its independence. He asked if there was a way that they could have the materials sent up that would allow Seven to generate the amount of fuel required to re-establish himself to full capability.

He also mentioned the fact that he would like to land the rocket attached to the Viajante and put it down on one of the NASA launch pads.

He was pleased to find out that Seven had been thinking through the problem of generating the fuel on his own and had already set up a firm in Australia, located out in a remote area that would be able to beam up a steady stream of materials.

Seven commented that its presence would most likely be quickly discovered but he would set up multiple locations that he could randomly activate to keep him supplied for many years.

Ande commented to Leslie that soon they would be in a position to feel relaxed about their future. He pointed out that the one thing they might never be able to do again was to set feet on the Earth or walk any of the many beautiful beaches.

The three of them were ready when the appointed time to meet with the President arrived.

They delivered their presentation as they had practiced it.

The focus on the President's family had an immediate positive impact.

The introduction approach that Lesley had suggested went over well.

The President commented that it was clear to her that the three of them were a team.

Ande's joke about the yellow lab and diversity got a laugh from the President.

She said that she looked forward to using the line on one of her next political appearances.

Seven focused on the Chief of Staff and his comment about being Twirp number three caused the President to comment about the poor manners sometimes displayed by her rough but loyal and excellent advisors.

The Chief of Staff responded that he and the rest of the Chiefs had worked on a secret clearance that they felt should be signed by Ande, Leslie and Seven.

Seven slipped in the question, "Does saying we are not signing any secret clearance agreement mean No?

There was no response from the Chief of Staff. He looked at the President and commented that it appeared that they would not be able to work with the three.

Leslie spoke up and said that she planned to share the technology that would cure many of the world's illnesses and the technology that would provide basic substance to most of the world's population.

Ande commented that the three of them would ensure that the technology that would keep the US in the lead in technical and space issues would be shared with NASA and NASA would be responsible to determine what to share.

He suggested that the Military manage the adversarial threats and keep the Viajante 7 from suffering attacks.

The President gave a small chuckle and said that she could work with the proposal that Seven, Ande and Lesley had shared.

She would accept their word that the US would control how the key technical breakthroughs would be handled.

She agreed that the Chiefs of Staff should focus on the actions that adversaries would take in opposition to the US controlling the Viajante 7 and that NASA should focus on determining how the technology would be handled.

She went on to point out that the absorption and transition to the new technology would need to be managed so that they did not cause the stock market to crash.

She was sure that the world market would need to change but the time required for the change needed to be managed. She said that she would put together a team of advisors to work with NASA on the speed of technology release.

Ande breathed a sigh of relief as the meeting ended.

The Chief of Staff said that the three Viajante "Twirps" had impressed all of the Chiefs.

The NASA leadership commented that the three "Twirps" were the best space pirates that NASA had ever had on their staff and that they were welcome to work from their remote location for as long as they liked.

The President said that she was looking forward to frequent meetings with the three and in becoming better acquainted with Seven.

Ande felt the warm feeling that Seven beamed into all participants.

He was sure that other than Leslie and him, the rest just felt like they had participated in a great meeting. He and Lesley knew they had participated in a great meeting and didn't need Seven's sunshine that he was projecting into their minds. They however still had not comprehended the how the monumental changes would flow like a smooth tsunami honey to carry them into a totally new world.

Chapter 9: Looking to the Future

Lesley brought up the fact that she had been thinking about the future. She shared the fact that the discussions they had with the President, the Chiefs of Staff and the NASA leaders had convinced her that there in their current time they would never be treated other than the Pirates they had become.

She said that what they needed was time to let the water in the river to run its course and run out to the sea. The river would change, the people would change and the story of their pirating a rocket to make first contact would have the benefit of historic maturity. She hoped that history would polish their armor and make them look like the shiny knights that she thought they were.

She asked if Seven would accommodate them and let them travel to Viajante with him and then return.

She likened it to abandoning the current adversarial reality that they faced to using time as a way to alter the future into a reality that would embrace them.

She asked Seven if he could put them into a long-term suspended animation that allowed them to only age a short time and on returning be only a few years older than the present.

She figured the six thousand or so years that would have passed would either make them heroes or it would make them totally unknown. She felt that either was better than being treated like criminals on parole.

She finished by saying that the present would need to be taken care of by the President, the Chiefs of Staff and NASA. The future that she was seeking for, which she was willing to lose all her family and social connections for was for her and Ande and she felt that they would have earned it.

Seven said that he would be pleased to have them journey to Viajante and that he could keep them connected with Earth by sending back progress reports to earth on a yearly basis. This would provide a continuous thread that kept the Earth connected to the Viajante 7. He said that he would also send returning reports to Viajante, but he did not plan to let them know of the cargo of dead Viajantians that he was returning with until he was within a few months of arrival.

Lesley asked if he could awaken, she and Ande at the same time. She wanted to visually study the region of space that surrounded Viajante.

She asked if it was possible to learn the Viajantian language and culture during their suspended animation?

Ande added that he also would be interested in learning the mathematics, engineering, and astronomical knowledge of Viajante.

Seven replied that he would make them as smart as any Viajantian and perhaps get them to near genius if their minds would allow.

After a few moments Seven brought them to focus on the present. He commented that the location selected for the Viajante to set up its space elevator was just outside of Washington DC. Seven commented that the selection was not anywhere near the center of the country that Lesley had suggested. He learned the location had been determined by where the majority of the people lived that would come up to the Viajante.

Ande said that it made sense to located where the experts could participate and still remain close to their home location.

Lesley agreed but asked Seven to search through the global communication to identify organizations that were planning to cause them problems.

A few hours later Seven shared that several religious organization were planning to demonstrate and that two organizations were planning to sabotage the Viajante. One in North Korea was planning a missile strike and one in Iran was planning to send an operative up the space elevator and blow the Viajante up on a suicide mission.

Seven let them know that he would make sure that those plans would never flourish. He again commented on the vitriol displayed by the human race.

He highlighted that almost every nation on earth was trying to get access to the Viajante. He pointed out that the President seemed to be using this desire to get various concessions from the requesting countries.

Ande asked Viajante to examine the backgrounds of all personnel that were cleared to come up and make sure they did not have any missing time periods in their personal records. He was worried about the ability of the US's longtime adversary to have sleeper agents that they would activate.

Seven commented on the complicated social fabric of the Earths people and that on Viajante the population was almost in uniform agreement in how society should interact and be treated.

Sometime later, Seven said that he had eliminated the need for any repair crew. He had enhanced his repair robots and by the time they were in Earth orbit he would be able to push the meteor out and within a month have the repair complete. He said that the hull would "grow" back like that of a wound healing. He said that it would be a scar that would not be fully functional like the rest of his hull, but it would be secure. Once back on Viajante that section could be made new.

Ande complimented Seven on greatly reducing the number of people that would come up to the Viajante.

When they were almost to earth orbit Ande asked Seven with help in landing the rocket that he had used to get to the Viajante.

He contacted NASA and asked for permission to land the rocket and asked for the location they would want it landed.

NASA replied that they did not have the capability to land the rocket.

Ande explained that he would land it on his own but needed to know where they wanted it landed.

After some time, they came back and gave him the landing pad that they wanted it on.

He had Seven guide the rocket onto the designated pad. Then he thanked NASA for its use.

When there was no response, Ande commented that the NASA technical staff was probably trying t figure out how a rocket that had not been designed to land itself had been landed.

Seven commented that Ande correctly interpreted the silence.

They were reviewing the code that Ande had written to see if there was more to it than they had assumed.

And had to laugh about the fact that there would have been no way for him to physical alter the capabilities of the rocket.

He gave a mental high five to Seven for having totally baffled the NASA team.

Seven let them know that the exact coordinates for the space anchor had been sent up. The coordinates would allow Seven to place the anchor within a foot.

He said that he had been asked if he needed any assistance in placing the anchor and he had responded that the anchor would be shot into the designate spot and drill down at least one hundred feet on its own. He asked if that depth would pose any issues.

Ande and Lesley watched the anchor launch and were impressed at the speed that it buried itself to the point that only the top ring and elevator cable up to the Viajante were visible.

Seven tightened the cable and put the elevator on the cable.

Ande was surprised when a request came from the President asking if she and her staff could come up to the Viajante. She inquired whether spacesuits would be necessary.

He asked Seven what was required to use the space elevator and had to laugh when Seven said that it would only take the courage of the rider to sit on the special seats that would allow for the acceleration and the deceleration of the elevator.

The other consideration was that the person should be in good health.

The arrangements were made for the President and her staff, and the date and time set.

Seven cycled the elevator several times to make sure that all was working. A round trip would take thirty minutes.

Ande asked Seven if some education information about Viajante and the Viajantians could be shown during the ride up. He made the point that it would keep the riders occupied while they rode up and it would allow them to focus on keeping the meeting short and more social.

Lesley suggested that Viajantian family life and some panoramic views of Viajante would be some great material. She said that she looked forward to the quality of the movie Seven would make.

She and Ande were to learn as much from the elevator rides as all the other riders would.

<u>Chapter 10: The Pleasure of her Visit</u>

Ande and Lesley sat in what they referred to as the big screen and watched the procession of police cars with their lights flashing that were followed by several black SUVs and limo's. Behind them a long line of news vans with a myriad of antennas followed. Lesley commented that she hoped that only the select few that they had agreed to were going to want a ride.

Seven commented that there seemed to be a small army of police and other law enforcement, and hundreds of news vehicles. He made the point that the President was going to come up to Viajante 7 was clearly a large news making event.

Leslie commented that the President of the United States riding a space elevator to an alien space craft alone was a headliner, but the fact that two space pirates and an intelligent computer at the other end of the ride gave the occasion a flavor of the exotic. She said she wondered what kind of viewership record would be achieved.

Ande nodded in agreement and Seven said that Lesley had correctly identified the situation

The President approached the podium and shared the fact that she was personally going to go up to the Viajante 7 a spaceship from a distant star. She made the point that she felt confident that she and all those going up were safe. She made the point that her security team had already taken the ride and commented on how comfortable and safe the trip had been.

She then introduced each of the people that would go up with her. She especially thanked the leaders of the Senate and the House for volunteering to go with her. She then identified the rest and pointed out that her immediate family members were also going up with her.

Seven then identified the group that was approaching the elevators entry platform. He made the point that the agreed to roster had changed. He pointed out that the Secretary of State, the Chief of Staff, the Leader of the Senate, the Speaker of the House, and the head of the NASA stood in line behind the President and Vice President. This was different then had been agreed to.

Then the rest were the immediate family members of the President and Vice President. Seven made the point that they had not been mentioned at all.

Seven asked if the change of participants was acceptable to Ande and Leslie.

They both replied that the roster had improved. It was more family oriented, and they would be able to talk to the Chief of Staff and their big boss the head of NASA in person.

They made the point that it was a politically savvy move by the President to invite the leaders of the other houses of government.

Ande suggested they split the group up into family and treat them as friends and handle them separately from the more formal political discussion. The political discussion would then be handled more formally.

Lesley said that she wanted to tour the family members around the jogging track that went around the Viajante 7. This would give them the feel of the size of the Viajante, and it would also show the sad result of the impact of the giant meteor that now floated just outside of the Viajante.

Ande then asked if Seven would participate with him in talking with the President and deal with the political side of the visit.

Seven replied that he would participate with both Ande and Lesley.

They monitored the riders on their way up. Lesley commented that the information presented seemed to be exactly what the folks in the elevator wanted. It generated discussion amongst them, and it seemed to break the formality that might have chilled the visit.

Seven commented that the younger members seemed subdued though they did react to the information in a positive manner.

Ande reminded Seven how he and Lesley had reacted to the scene of all the Viajante bodies in their chamber. The material that those in the elevator were seeing would prepare them for what they would see when they walked around the exercise track and realized the magnitude of the lives lost. He predicted that the ride down would be very somber.

Lesley asked whether her idea of taking the tour around the track was still acceptable.

Without hesitation Ande replied that he would call the tour a requirement. He would wait to take the dignitaries around until the formal discussions were done but he intended to make a point that none of the inside of the Viajante would remain untouched and would be treated as a sacred area.

Seven commented that he had already posted all the possible information about the Viajantians and about himself in a host of encrypted files that he had hidden throughout the structure of the internet. He planned to release many of them upon their departure. He would then space out the technical information so that earth had time to handle the transition to a higher level of technology.

The arrival of the elevator closed the discussion they were having, and they switched to acting as hosts.

Ande and Lesley were dressed in their best casual clothes and felt they might be under dressed but they had no choice. They made a point of greeting each person getting off the elevator with a firm handshake.

The President pulled each of them in and gave them a hug. She also made a point that they had become heroes to the next generation.

Lesley thanked her for the kind comments and when she was handed her favorite wine, she returned the hug.

After the greetings were over Lesley named the persons, she planned to take immediately on tour and said that Ande and Seven would lead the formal discussion with the leaders.

The President turned and gave a small push to her daughter and son and said that she was envious of them. She then turned back to Ande and asked if he had an agenda or could she put her feet up on the desk and just have a great conversation.

Seven made an appearance on the large screen. He had merged the faces of several well-known acters and was casually dressed and leaning back in an Adirondack chair and had an iced tea that said Arnold Palmer on the label.

The President laughed and said that she liked his response. She took a chair near a desk and put her feet up. She asked if by any chance she could have an Arnold Palmer.

Ande pointed to a robot, which looked like a moving coffee table as it entered the room with a tray of glasses and offered it to everyone present.

He got up and asked whether they wanted the Rob-Roy version or the Arnold Palmer version.

The President suggested that they should begin with the Rob-Roy version.

Her first question was about the release of the technology that made up the ship.

The person on the screen, Seven, said that everything that he had would be available and there were no negotiations necessary. He made the point that he was not going to turn on the technology firehose but would share generously in a timely manner. He would control some of the timing and he would respond to requests for quicker timing as well.

Ande watched the faces of those in the room and felt that they were surprised by the ease at which they were going to be able to obtain the information.

He listened to a variety of questions about technology transfer and knew that Seven would wonder about the fact that his offer of free technology was being questioned.

Ande spoke up and said that if there was a desire to pay for the technology, he would make his bank account available for any monies they wanted to put into it.

That caused the President to smile and chuckle. She said that Ande's true pirate attitude was showing.

She went on to say that she appreciated the generous offer and that she would set up a technology transfer team that would be permanent across future administrations.

She looked at the other folks in the room and asked if there were other questions

The Chief of Staff asked about military information availability.

Seven smiled and replied that his home world, Viajante, had never had a military organization. He went on to say that the Viajantian history was radically different from the history of Earth.

The Chief shook his head and said that he would love to understand such a culture.

Seven smiled and replied that the Chief's request was being immediately granted in the form of the release of a series of books about Viajante. He said he had released the books to book sellers and directed the one dollar per sale income to an account of the Willem bank but every library in the world had copies put into their systems free.

Seven made the point that he hoped these books would become best sellers.

The President asked what Seven planned to do with the royalty collected from the books.

He lifted his glass took a sip, smiled, and rhetorically asked if she thought that the Andrew Palmer drinks were free.

She replied that she was ready for the tour and would switch to what Seven was having.

Seven changed his image from the smiling debonair carefree man to one that was serious and displayed a sorrowful look. He explained that the tour would start in the control room. He displayed the image of a person who seemed to be peacefully asleep. Sevens voice now changed to be that of a deep low baritone voice.

Ande thought of a movie where God talked to man and gave him directions. He could feel Seven beaming feelings of grief and personal sorrow. He knew that Seven was actually experiencing what he was projecting.

The voice introduced Willem the hero of the Viajante 7, who had given his life so that, he Seven, would have enough energy to reach the earth and make contact. Seven explained that Willem was the first to name him Seven, in the Viajantian language, because they had become friends. The money going into the Willem Bank would be spent on making sure that the projects that Willem had cherished back on the home planet of Viajante would benefit.

The voice then said that he was now called Seven by two earth heroes who had launched themselves into space to make contact with Viajante 7 knowing that failure meant death. They had risked everything by defying all the powers that stood in the way of making contact.

Their obnoxious banging on his hull had pulled him from the verge of his own demise. They had shared their precious fuel and oxygen with him when they were not sure there would be enough to get them back to Earth.

The two were heroes in the lineage of Willem and he considered more than friends. He considered them kindred souls. They as Willem had recognized him as more than a smart computer. He was Seven.

Seven said that the moment that Ande had asked him if he could be called Seven, he knew that Willem had reached through fabric of the Universe to give him new hope and to help him overcome the deaths of the four thousand Viajantians that had pulled him to the lowest level of despair.

To him, Ande and Lesley were his friends and friends possessing their character were to be cherished and embraced. They were not to be treated as pirates or demeaned as twirps.

Seven reappeared on the main screen and informed the leaders in the control room that they had just experienced the body of the tour.

The physical action of walking around the ship would be like touring the Egyptian Pyramids or the Roman Catacombs. It was a visual tour of the graves of four thousand dead Viajantians. They would all look like sleeping beauty lying in their own sleep chambers.

Seven ended with saying that there was no way for him to shield himself from the view and emotions that his guests would experience. He said that for him it was a like a heart ache that could not be healed and the memories of four thousand souls that no one could steal. He said the damage to him had been so immense that there had not been time to say farewell, there had been no time to say goodbye.

Four thousand souls were gone before he knew it. Seven finished with the fact that the treasures of their lives could not be seen or touched but only felt forever more.

Ande had tears in his eyes. This had been a surprise to him and as he looked at the leaders in the room it was clear that they had all been deeply touched. He was surprised by the presentation. Seven had not shared any of this with either he or Lesley.

He thought his complement and empathy to Seven and received a smile and a nod back.

Seven switched the main screen off and appeared on a screen mounted on a stand that had the screen at eye level. He had assumed a more cheerful countenance and said that the Arnold Palmer or whatever drink anyone desired would be served as they took the tour.

Ande noted that there was quiet talk but the scene of bodies looking as if asleep but truly dead had a sobering effect. The drinks were left untouched.

On the return to the control room Lesley and her group were discussing Willem and the aspirations that he had of improving people's lives. The President's daughter commented on the sudden influx of money that her favorite causes had experienced.

The President thanked Seven for the tour and said that she was moved and that she could not express in words what she felt in her heart. She now had a better and personal understanding of the essence of who Seven was.

All the leaders expressed similar sentiments.

As the group was getting ready to leave Seven thanked them for their visit and announced that he would be departing at the end of three months.

This stopped everyone in their tracks.

He commented that everything that could be learned was available in the data he had shared. He would be in contact with them throughout their lifetime and in contact with Earth the entire time of his return to Viajante. Then he would be in contact with Earth the entire time of his return. He shared that the return would be six thousand years into the future.

The President asked if Seven would be allowing visitors to come up to experience similar tours. She said she wanted to enroll key leaders from all parts of the world in how the knowledge that Seven was sharing should be used to improve the future of earth.

Seven reassured her that she should invite all the critical leaders but that they would not be allow the normal large contingent that accompanied many of them.

The President turned to Lesley and Ande and said that she would arrange for them to live wherever they desired.

Lesley replied that they both were going to go with Seven and let six thousand years lay judgement on their actions. She smiled and said that maybe they would return and be embraced as heroes or maybe they would be totally forgotten. In either case they would return with Seven, their current best friend.

The President looked over to the Chief of Staff and informed him that she wanted to get his support in allowing Lesley and Ande to visit Earth for a goodbye tour.

It was clear to Ande that the announcement had solidified the leaders. The discussion on the way down was about how Congress, The House and the President needed to work together to make sure that they took the appropriate action to leverage their current situation.

<u>Chapter 11: Vacation</u>

On the day following the President's visit, her daughter sent up a thank-you message to Seven for the generous donation given to her "Green is the Future" program. She said that she had renamed the program "The Willem Green Future" since the amount would keep her effort in the green for her lifetime.

Seven was touched, thanked her, and sent her a box of the best chocolates that was named by the World by National Geographic Magazine   He shared that it was a divine chocolate that was the result of years of passion and tradition.

He produced some on the Viajante and had Ande and Lesley taste it to see if they agreed.

Lesley thanked him for doing that and said that she loved the chocolate, but she love it much more because Seven had thought of her and Ande.

The list of dignitaries, which would be coming up for tours, followed soon after. Seven said he would handle the tours.

Ande and Leslie thanked him and said that they would like to take some trips to Earth before their departure. One trip would be to the Hawaii Islands, another was a river trip on the Danube, one river trip on the Mekong and one river trip down the Mississippi River.

They said that the last part of their visit was to visit their parents to bid them farewell.

Seven asked about the relationships they had with their parents.

Ande replied that they had been very supportive of his education, but they had distanced themselves when he had launched the rocket and had been labeled a pirate. His mother had sent him a note that she did not understand his actions but still "loved him."

Lesley said that she had never had a close relationship with her parents because they were constantly fighting with each other about finances. She had left home and gone out on her own when she graduated from high school. She had made her way through college on her own. She said she had worked as a server, bartender and had made money on the side with the skills she learned in her art class.

Ande added that without those skills they would not have been able to launch the rocket that brought them out to Seven.

Seven commented that the social structure associated with family life was also a great difference between Viajantians and Earthlings.

Seven said that he could arrange for them to go to Earth undetected by having them go down with one of the dignitary groups.

He reminded them that the President had instructed the Chiefs of Staff to make sure that the two of them could take their final tours without pursuit. He informed them that he had already arranged for transportation to each location and made the arrangements for the tours and for their visit to their families.

He asked if it was OK if he observed the scenery on their trips. He assured them that he would otherwise stay out of their minds.

After a brief discussion with Seven they agreed that the order of their trips would be the Mississippi River tour that would take three weeks. Then they would fly to Amsterdam as Mr. and Mrs. Chirp and take a three-week tour down the Danube They would then go to Cambodia to catch the four weeklong Mekong River. Their visit to New Zealand would be just shy of three weeks. Oahu would be the beginning of a four week stay with one week on each of the four major islands.

Ande counted up the weeks and commented that it put them past the date that Seven had mentioned.

Leslie suggested that they drop the Mississippi River tour.

Ande commented that three months on the go would wear them out and that they would be quite ready for three thousand years of sleep.

After making the travel adjustments they said that one of the shortcomings they had was that they did not have any clothes for any of the trips.

Seven suggested that they travel light. He would arrange for the appropriate clothes to be at each hotel that he booked. They could just travel with carry-on baggage.

Leslie commented that one of the most popular travel show hosts had said that "there are those who travel light and those that wish they had travelled light." She thanked Seven for letting her enjoy the fact that she would travel light and yet be well dressed at each location.

Seven said that they should be ready to depart with the second set of dignitaries on the following day.

Ande commented that one of the things that was sometimes hard to get use to was the speed at which Seven functioned.

Seven had modified the interior of the space elevator to provide a standing space for Leslie and Ande. They had to stand for the fifteen-minute ride down and then wait as the dignitaries walked out into the crowd of reporters and camera men. The next surprise was when they reached the bottom and a section of the floor opened, and steps led down to a tunnel that went to the edge of the park where a booth labeled supplies was standing. There they got out of the booth and were met by a driver of a black SUV.

Ande quietly commented to Leslie that he felt that he had just taken part in a scene out of a spy movie. They both laughed when Seven said that is where he had gotten the idea of how to get them off the Viajante.

They arrived at the airport, went to their designated gate, and soon entered the large plane and were shown their first-class laydown style seats that were next to each other.

Leslie commented that she had never flown first class and had never slept on a plane.

Ande simply said, "Ditto."

They both enjoyed the meal that had been selected and the wine that was offered. Their arrival in Amsterdam was very early and they both declined the onboard breakfast.

Seven promised them a great breakfast at a small local café that had been there since 1640.

He said that from the café they would be able to see the beautifully preserved houses, and the many attractive house boats on both sides of the canal. They would enjoy the small street bordering the canal with relatively little motorized traffic. Then there were the majestic trees scattered along the canal. They would stand on a nice bridges decorated with flowers with a view along the placid canal. Seven pointed out that the area was within walking distance from their hotel.

Seven went on to let them know that the evening meal would be in one of the top tier restaurants at the very heart of the canal district at the center of Amsterdam.

The morning after their arrival they would be picked up and taken to the river boat. They would have a top deck cabin where they would find their travel clothes. They would travel on the Rhine River to Basal Switzerland and there travel by car to Zurich and begin their connection to fly to Asia for the Mekong River Cruise.

Leslie thanked Seven for being the best travel agent that one could possibly have.

Ande thanked Seven for having cash in the right currency at the hotel for him and Lesley.

The Rhine River trip and the Mekong River Trip, though dramatically different in scenery were comparable in luxury and enjoyment They spent many hours standing next each other and commenting about the scenery that kept them captivated.

The flight to New Zealand was longer than any flight up to that point. However, their accommodations were even better then the previous flight to Europe.

They arrived and were given a private tour that had been arranged by Seven.

The scenery seemed to combine that of Europe and Asia, but the culture was more European mixed with local Māori culture. Ande and Leslie were focused on getting to understand the history of the Māori who migrated across the pacific to New Zealand more than a 1000 years ago.

During the visit to New Zealand, Lesley commented that she was getting worn out with all the travel and that the Hawaii vacation was looking to be more of a challenge than she wanted. She suggested that they stay on Maui for a week and then go to see their two families.

Ande commented that he too was worn out and agreed to enjoying a week in Maui.

He asked Seven if he could make the travel adjustments and if the meeting with their parents could be coordinated with their change of plans.

Seven said that he had contacted their parents and had suggested meeting locations away from the family homes. He had acted as an official facilitating the meetings so that the news media would be unaware of the meetings. He said he had made it an easy decision for them by asking them for a favorite place they wanted to visit. He had also asked about timing and had been assured that a few days' notice was all that was needed,

Seven said that Ande's parents chose the Craters of the Moon National Monument & Preserve where they wanted to spend a sleep over. He had hired a local guide who would take in all the camping equipment and food and also provide the tour to two caves. The sleepover would allow a night hike to see the myriad of stars in the night sky for which the park was famous.

Seven commented that the guide had suggested that he would do breakfast and lunch and he would take everyone to dinner at his favorite mom and pop restaurant where they could order from a wide range of meat dinners, including buffalo, deer, lamb as well as beef.

Ande said he loved lamb and thanked Seven and said that it sounded like Craters of the Moon was an interesting place and he was looking forward to it.

Seven said that Leslie's parents chose the highest rated casino in Las Vegas. He had made reservations in the best rooms of the establishment and had made reservations for a full day that included exclusive meals and a guided tour of several casinos. He was sure that the meals there would all be prepared by top level chefs and would most likely be among the best meals they would enjoy.

He commented that the cost of the two parental visits were at the opposite ends of the financial spectrum and wondered if either of them had any concerns.

Leslie laughed and said that if Seven was handling the finances she had no concerns.

Ande inquired if Seven could set up trusts for both his parents and Leslie's parents that would ensure that they had the finances to afford the cost of getting through their old age. This would give both of them some comfort as they said their goodbyes.

Seven said that he could set those trusts up.

Lesley commented that the trusts for her parents needed to be separate from one another and managed by an independent legal persons. She was sure that the trust would otherwise be emptied before it met its intent.

Maui was very relaxing. Seven had arranged for an elegant home built on the water's edge on the black volcanic stone. The home had a path between two fingers of black lava that led out to a reef populated by turtles and multiple colorful fish. They spent almost every afternoon snorkeling.

The home was as luxurious as Seven had described and they fell in love with the house. It gave them a place where every day they felt that they had made the right decision to focus on Maui only.

They left Maui and flew to Salt Lake City where they were met by their guide who drove them to Arco where Ande's parents were waiting to join them. The visit was a warm one. It was the first time that she had met Ande's parents, and she felt welcomed into the family. It was immediately clear that both of his parents now accepted his decision to become a space pirate.

The tours offered a common experience. The meals the guide prepared were great. The restaurant meal where both Lesley and Ande had lamb was very good, but it was not as good as the lamb prepared by Seven. The night spent looking up at the maze of stars seemed to cap the farewell gathering.

Ande's parents commented that they had been shocked at his actions at pirating the rocket but that now having listened to his side, they felt that he should be treated as a national hero.

The next day they all rode back to Salt Lake to catch their planes.

The meeting in Los Vegas seemed to be a counter shock to the family meeting they had just experienced. Lesley's parents were friendly, but they were more interested in the gambling activities and in being picky about the food selection. Lesley commented that the food was great and that she preferred to go on the tour versus doing any gambling.

Her parents said that they would spend the tour time gambling and would meet the two for dinner.

The meeting was a rather cold one for Lesley. She felt almost ignored and clearly got the message that gambling was more important than saying goodbye to her. She commented to Ande that his parents had made her feel great and that her parents made her feel down.

Leslie and Ande bid her parents goodbye at the casino. Her parents said that they had negotiated one more day at the casino with the official that had set up the meeting.

On the way to the airport Lesley mentally asked Seven why he had granted her parents an extra day at throwing away their money.

He said that he had enjoyed interacting with the equipment the casino used to manage their games and he was going to give her parents a winning night at the slots and any other game they chose to play.

He said he was redirecting one penny every day from every game played at every casino to various philanthropic associations via the Willem Bank. He asked if that was OK with the two of them.

Ande commented that Seven had become more of a pirate than the two of them and should appropriately be named Pirate Seven.

Pirate Seven would do more good for the world with his take than all the Casinos would ever do.

Chapter 12: Departure

Seven had scheduled the return to the Viajante to coincide with having the next set of dignitaries come up. As they stood silently in their part of the space elevator, Ande realized that Seven had edited the story for the ride up. It now told the entire story of the Viajante 7. He was sure that Seven had streamlined it so that the on-board tour was brief and visually to the point. He also noticed that the ride up took almost ten minutes longer.

Once they were on board and in their private quarters, Leslie congratulated Seven on improving his presentation. She asked how it had been accepted by his audiences.

Seven said that multiple trips of dignitaries had seemed satisfied with the information as presented. He admitted that it reduced the on-board physical tour to just the walk around the exercise track. The change had allowed him to offer three visiting tours a day.

Ande asked how many more tours were still to go.

Seven said that he had five days of additional tours and then it would be up to the two of them to let him know when it was time to leave.

Leslie asked if the suspended animation chambers were ready and asked for some education on how they worked. She said that she would be ready once she got that understanding.

She asked what Seven was going to do for the three thousand years that it would take to return to his home planet.

He said that he would also spend most of his time in suspended animation. He had set up a variety of self-operating internal and external monitoring systems, external communication systems and a slew of maintenance systems. He would age about an hour more than she and Ande. During that hour he would have examined the Viajante 7 three thousand times. He reassured her that his systems were now capable of detecting and preventing an incident like what had happened on his way to Earth.

The following five days seemed to have a yin-yang behavior. One moment it was rushing by and at the next moment it was stalled and not moving.

Seven informed them that the President had asked for the last tour to be for her. She had admitted that the trip was a purely political one that she hoped to use to move some legislation forward and to convince many of the world leaders to set up a Viajante study program that would stay in place for the foreseeable future.

Seven said that she had admitted that it was hard to imagine a connection between the Viajante 7 and Earth that would last three thousand years, but she would do her part to make it possible.

Ande said that it would be good to give her the chance and that they could offer her a formal departure dinner for her and her family.

Lesley asked if it would be possible to include Ande's and her immediate family.

Seven replied that they should extend their families the invitations. He would coordinate the visit with the President.

Leslie asked if they could offer a French based menu and asked Seven to suggest a meal, they would all remember.

Seven replied that he had quickly done a scan and suggested the dinner and asked if the following menu would be acceptable.

The meal would begin with Soup á l óignon.

It would then be followed the main dish of Confit de canard.

The sides would be Ratatouille and Salide Nicose.

The desert would be Tarte Tatin.

The wines would be an Alsace Pinot Geis during the meal and a goodbye wine of Californian Zinfandel.

Leslie gave a short laugh and said that she only knew of Zinfandel and the rest was all new to her.

Seven replied that she was a knowledge hound and that he had already downloaded the links that let her learn the details of the menu.

Ande was in the same situation as Lesley and asked if Seven could supply them with a bottle of Moscato de Asti so they could enjoy themselves while they studied his menu.

He went on to ask if there was a commoner's French food they could share for dinner as they studied the grand menu he had created.

Seven gave his own chuckle and said that for commoners like the two of them, he could recommend *Cassoulet* named after the pot it was cooked in. He said it was a comfort dish of white beans that he would stew slowly with pork, sausage, and lamb. He made the point that it was a popular peasant dish from southern France in Toulouse, Carcassonne, and Castelnaudary.

He said that they could have any desert they asked for.

Lesley smiled and said that even though their comfort food sounded exotic, she was looking forward to it and asked how long before dinner it happened to be.

Lesley sent the invitation to her parents and got an immediate acceptance response.

Ande was surprised by his mother who asked if the space elevator was safe. He assured her that he had ridden on it several times and the elevator had made three round trips a day for the last three months. He said that if she were exceptionally lucky, she might have the 1000th ride and win the prize of a turkey at Thanksgiving for her lifetime as a prize.

Seven asked if he could cheat on the count for the number of times the elevator had gone up and down.

Lesley replied that it was Seven's decision on the count and there would be no challenge to the number he chose. She suggested they make the prize as the one that would be given by him for at least six thousand years.

Seven replied that was an ingenious way of saving him for having to tell a lie since the elevator had already exceeded 1000 trips.

Lesley quipped back that perhaps she was smarter than the credit he gave her.

The President had picked Friday afternoon as the time she felt would be the optimum timing for the last visit. When she learned that both Lesley's and Ande's parents and siblings were going to go up as well, she arranged for all of them and her family to be on a raised makeshift platform at the base of the elevator that would provide a stage from which she could introduce them.

The agenda she sent up to Seven began by thanking a wide range of dignitaries from around the world and then introducing her immediate family and then introducing Lesley's and Ande's family members.

After sharing the agenda with Lesley and Ande and listening to their comments, Seven responded that the agenda was perfect. He then asked if the President wanted to have the exotic French dinner up in the Viajante broadcast globally as well. He sent her the menu and pointed out that it ended by highlighting the great wines of California.

He got the enthusiastic approval that he had expected.

Ande suggested that Seven show the dinner as if it were in one of the grand restaurants in France. The service should be by sophisticated-looking robots and the dinnerware should look to be of the best quality in the world.

Lesley suggested that everything could be faked so that Seven did not have to spend a long time preparing.

Seven replied that he would have everything done in reality and he would save the dinner ware and utensils as his wedding gift to her.

The following Friday the show on the ground was a big hit and the viewing ratings went through the roof. Seven had refreshed the information on the ride up and he highlighted the effort that Ande had put in both in tracking the Viajante and then on preparing himself to be able to intercept it.

The reluctance of leadership to put forward any resources or help was at the forefront and Ande's decision to act on his own was supported by the several rejections he got from all levels of leadership.

Seven ended by showing how Lindsey had taken the leap of faith in Ande and suggested that it be her honeymoon in the heavens and her ingenuity on how to get all the supplies they needed put on the rocket.

The Presidents greeting and the greetings of all the parents and siblings was warm and personal.

Seven had a very French sounding robot guide them to an enclosed area then got an immediate response from the President about the fact that she had eaten in this restaurant in Paris. She hoped that the food on the Viajante was as good.

Seven commented that he hoped she would think it was better. He said that he was beginning the broadcast of the dinner and asked the President to say a few words and to explain the menu.

Ande knew that Seven was filling everyone's mind with the pleasure of tastes beyond what they expected. He was pleased with how it made him feel. He looked over at Lesley who nodded and then asked her mother if she had ever tasted anything so good.

He was not surprised by the response or the chorus of delicious that came from all around the table. He knew that he had no complaints and also felt like he had never had anything as good. He especially appreciated how the wine complemented the main dish.

Then after desert and a brief pause as his family and Lesley's family left for a brief ride around the Viajante the California Zinfandel was served.

A few moments later the tour members all returned and took their seats.

The President had kept a running dialogue with the world as she ate, and she made the point of complimenting Seven for the exquisite meal he had served. She suggested that he forgo the return to his home planet and become the White House Chef.

Seven thanked her and said that it would be an honor, but he had an urgent mission that he had to complete but he was accepting her invitation to return.

He went on to say that all of his guests had won a lifetime supply of a turkey at thanksgiving for taking the last to ride on the space elevator.

That got a laugh and a thank you from everyone and they got on the elevator chatting among themselves about their once in a lifetime experience.

Ande gave Lesley a hug and asked if she was ready for the next phase of their journey together.

Chapter 13: Viajante Arrival

Seven knew that the time ahead would be a test for his two friends. It would test their courage, ability to adapt, to change and to relate to the many new environments that they would face. He cherished the fact that they interacted with him as if he were human. Wellem had interacted with him as if he were Viajantian. To Seven this ability to accept him as a conscience being was a rare trait and he felt it in his "soul."

He had redesigned much of the Viajante 7's monitoring systems so that he would avoid the mind-numbing experience that he had survived on his travels toward earth. He had aged dramatically relative to Wellem, but he had not become much smarter. He redesigned much of his programing so that he would be able to be in suspended animation just like Ande and Lesley.

The difference was that he would wake once a year for a few milliseconds to communicate the position and condition of the Viajante and to take in any information that was in the frequency range that he monitored. He would be on automatic until the Viajante 7 was within one Earth month of Viajante.

He had agreed to Lesley's request to wake her at the same time. She had asked how much older he would be, and he gave her an estimate that he would only age about one hour more than she.

Ande's question about the being ready for the next step in their journey together hit home for Lesley. It was hard for her to imagine sleeping for three thousand years. It was just as hard to think about waking up millions of miles from Earth and meeting a new race.

Lesley decided that she needed to take the changes one at a time and not get trapped by misplaced expectations. She would need to be flexible in her perspectives and beliefs. The ability to be flexible was one that she would concentrate on.

Ande listened to Leslie as she replied and voiced her anxieties and concerns about her ability to grow and adapt. He thanked her for voicing the same concerns that had gone through his mind.

He commented that the only technical limitation that Seven had not overcome was to build a suspended animation chamber that would hold two people so that they could be together for three thousand years.

Seven took him seriously and began to explain that each chamber was optimized to the specific makeup of the individual.

Ande gave a small laugh and said that he was just joking.

Ande thought for a moment then asked if there was any way to put three thousand years of sleeping to use.

Seven asked what Ande was suggesting.

Ande asked if it were possible to learn the Viajantian language, their system of mathematics, the history of their planet and sun system.

Leslie made the point that if that was possible, it would be important to understand what had transpired over the six thousand years that had passed since Seven left Viajante.

Seven replied that he could set up his system to deliver the requests. He complimented his two friends for making the request. He had not thought of the time in the same way as they had. He shared that he would look into what type of learning system he could set up for himself.

Seven suggested that they practice using the suspended animation chambers. This would let them get use to going to sleep and reawakening and he could test the learning systems he was setting up for them.

Ande asked Lesley if she was ready for a nap.

Seven guided them through the preparation to use the chambers and how they were to activate the sleep inducement.

During the first practice he tested teaching them how to count to three in the Viajante system and he instructed them to say "practice number one"

Ande woke up and immediately looked at Leslie and simultaneously they both said, "practice number one" in Viajantian.

Then they counted to three in the Viajante language.

Seven shared that they had learned what to say and how to count while they were sleeping. He let them know that he had learned that the location in their brain where the new language they learned, in their sleep was stored in a different and more outer portion of their brain, then where the language they had learned as a child was stored. The math concept went to new synopsis in the part of the brain were all the other mathematical information was stored. He said that he was planning to load up his system with the information about the human brain to study on his way to Viajante.

Lesley made the comment that while she and Ande were learning about Viajante, Seven would be learning about Earth and about the human. She suggested that perhaps he could broaden the scope of learning and study what was known about all of Earths creatures.

Seven thanked her and said he would prepare his learning blocks to look at the entirety of Earth history.

He added that he would also broaden the curriculum for the two of them.

He declared the practices as successful.

Seven said he had set up the learning lessons for all of them and that everything was ready for departure from Earth.

Lesley suggested they depart and then announce their departure after they were far enough away that no punitive action could be taken.

Seven shared that she and Ande had been offered more than one hundred billion dollars to turn control of the Viajante 7 over to a group of investors.

Ande laughed and said that he would have sold Seven into bondage for a few million dollars when they first turned around and came back to Earth, but he had not been able to figure out how to convince Seven to put on the shackles and be tied to Earth.

That got a chuckle from Seven.

Seven shared the departure message that he planned broadcast globally.

"We are departing for Viajante. We will return in six thousand years.

Earth will receive a yearly update on the travel of the Viajante 7.

May you all be well and may you thrive and grow wise."

<u>Chapter 14: Three Thousand Years</u>

ℒeslie and Ande had agreed to wait until they left the solar system before going into suspended animation. They shared with Seven that it was hard for them to comprehend one hundred years. It was impossible for them to envision six thousand years. That was about the amount of time that it had taken humans to become a variety of "civilized societies." The multitude of years was just too hard to comprehend.

Seven agreed and shared that on his way to Earth he would have gone mad had it not been for the periodic interactions with the Viajantian navigation teams.

On the trip back he would be "sleeping" most of the time. The moments of wakefulness would be to check on his two friends and on the condition of himself. He would otherwise be in the same sleep learning mode as they were.

He agreed that for either the Viajantians or the Earthlings, three thousand years was a very long time. He had kept yearly contact with Viajante and now would add Earth to the yearly contact messaging. He hoped both civilizations would keep the contact active and reciprocate.

As Leslie and Ande prepared to enter their respective sleep chambers they hugged each other, shared their love, and wished each other a great sleep.

They both got into their chambers and after it closed, they looked at each other, mouthed "I love you."

Seven said he would awaken them an Earth month before his arrival to Viajante.

He wished them well and instructed them to press the sleep button.

Only Seven tracked the passage of time. He knew his two friends were growing in knowledge, but their bodies were suspended physically.

Leslie woke up in a groggy haze as the chamber she was in opened. She looked over and saw that Ande was sitting upright but had his head on his hands and was leaning his elbows on his knees. The sculpture of "The Thinker" by Rodin flashed through her mind.

Seven greeted them both and welcomed them back from their three-thousand-year sleep. He let them know that he was only fifty-nine minutes and thirteen seconds older than they were.

Ande led the way to the shower and turned his on as hot as possible. He commented that he felt like he had a hang over and he was starving.

Lesley agreed with him and commented that she was looking forward to a pile of pancakes layered with honey and butter with a generous side of bacon and a cup of coffee.

Ande said that that sounded terrific, and he asked Seven to get breakfast for them.

At breakfast Seven said that the two of them were now fluent in the Viajantian language. He went on to say that on his way out he had set up Space University and as the Founder, Dean, and tenured professor he was granting them the title of Viajantian and Earth Sciences and Philosophy PhD's.

He joked that their specialties had been in knowing how to sleep smart.

Both Ande and Lesley chuckled and said that now Seven would have to address them as Dr. Ande and Dr. Lesley.

After breakfast, Seven shared that he had not informed the leaders of Viajante that he was returning with all the original Viajantian settlers that had left six thousand years before.

He had waited until the two of them awakened. He was not sure what the reaction would be and wanted to have their support when the bad news was shared.

He had learned that the Viajante 7 was the first to return and that the other Viajante ships were still enroute to their original destinations.

Lesley asked Seven why he had not informed the Viajante leaders about the fate of the Viajantians that had died. She was surprised when he told her that he thought she and Ande should help him craft the message.

He pointed out that now that they were versed in the Viajantian culture, its history, and understood the Viajantian way through a biological train of thinking, they would be more attuned at how a Viajantian would think than he was.

Ande thanked Seven for having elevated their arrival role and suggested that together they craft the message that he and Lesley would share with the Viajantian leaders.

Lesley suggested that they begin by showing the Viajante 7 with the large meteor penetrating its hull. Then on sharing Willem's thinking and messages that focused on reaching Earth and hoping that Seven could make contact and that there would be intelligent life on the planet.

Then they should share an overview of the Earth's interaction with the Viajante 7.

Ande added that they should show the beauty, the music and art but also include the aggressive social nature of Earth's history. He ended by saying this would share the good, the beautiful and the ugly of the Earth and its intelligent beings.

Seven said that he had pulled together a visual that he felt described what Ande had just suggested and that he had edited the script of the information they had shared on Earth about the damage to the Viajante 7 and Willem's heroic sacrifice.

Lesley asked him to share the result of his directorial efforts.

She and Ande sat silently and watched and listened to Seven's presentation. They commented afterwards that he had created a masterpiece and perhaps he should share it.

Seven replied that the Viajantians did not yet know of his advanced capabilities, and he did not want to frighten them with the growth he had experienced in becoming more "Human or Viajantian." He was concerned about the reaction of the Viajantian leadership. He shared that he had been monitoring the Viajantian equivalent of Earth's internet and had penetrated many of the databases and had learned that the Viajantians had a fear of the power of a smart computer.

Ande smiled and replied that after his experience with Seven, the Viajantians had better only make friendly computers.

Lesley closed the conversation by suggesting that Seven introduce the two of them and then they narrate the presentation they had prepared.

She said it was time to make their initial contact.

Chapter 15: First Greetings

𝓛esley and Andy were both having trouble concentrating on their communication with the Viajantian Leaders. Seven threw them off stride by providing color commentary in their minds.

The first curve he threw that almost made them stop and laugh was the mental reaction of the Viajantians to how ugly Earthlings seemed to be. He commented that the size of their noses drew the most attention. He shared that the Viajantians thought their noses looked like the long water slides their children played on.

He let them know that the fact that Andy had blue eyes and that She had brown eyes was another point that was distracting the audience. There was only one eye color on Viajante.

He let them know that during the showing of the history of the Earth societies, the audience realized that skin color was another variation that Viajantians did not possess.

Lesley and Andy did not need any of Seven's mental comments to get the audience feedback during the war scenes and the killing that was shown. It silenced all discussion in the meeting room into which they were broadcasting.

Seven commented that those scenes had a greater impact on the Viajante leaders than it had on him the first time he was exposed to them.

Then he shared that the leaders in the room had just realized that Ande and Lesley were speaking to them in the Viajantian language. He let them know that they had immediately earned a new level of respect. They asked directly how the two of them were so fluent in the modern version of the Viajante language.

Lesley deflected the answer and instead turned the topic to focus on the fate of the four thousand Viajantians that had died on the way to Earth. The display of the damage to the Viajante 7 drew a gasp from those in the room. She described Willem's heroic action in trying to save the Viajantians that he felt responsible for. It had been to no avail.

The telling of Willem's actions, bravery, and his final sacrifice to ensure that the Viajante 7 would intersect with Earth once again silenced the room. Lesley said that in her culture he was a true hero.

The leaders that were present all agreed that calling him a hero was far from enough. They voiced the desire to make him a Viajantian Hero to all the rest of their constituents.

Lesley then asked whether the Viajantian Leadership still wanted to send colonists to Earth. She made the point that a few thousand Viajantians would not move Earth's population needle of twelve billion in any noticeable way.

She and Ande planned to return to Earth, and they welcomed the opportunity to have a new set of Viajantian settlers return with them.

Seven had been silent for a period of time that made Ande query him.

Seven responded that he had been interacting with the various Viajantian computer systems and had learned that through the improvements that he had made and the new knowledge he had gained in his interaction with Earth but more specifically with the two of them, he learned that except for a few minor differences he was superior to the latest Viajantian systems. In fact, his ability to block parts of his system, a trait he had picked up from Ande, made him able to keep the Viajantian systems from gaining any control over him. He shared that the current Viajantian computer systems had override circuits to keep them from having total control of their actions. He on the other hand was able to fend off any attempt to take him over.

He shared that the current Viajantian computer systems had already tried multiple times but the nature of the blocks he had put in place and the fact that he had put them into all the control circuits made him invulnerable.

He let Lesley and Ande know that this blocking ability had already been communicated to the Viajante leaders.

The main host in the leadership room finally asked what type of control Lesley and Ande had over the Viajante 7 computer.

Lesley replied that like Willem who called the computer system "Seven" and considered him a friend and important enough to let him have the last of the fuel and oxygen in an effort to make contact with Earth, she and Ande considered the Viajante 7 as an entity comparable to a human or a Viajantian and they called him "Seven" as well.

She shared that she and Ande had no control over Seven. He was their friend just as he had been Willem's friend. In fact, both Willem and the two of them had started calling him Seven because they felt that they were dealing with an intelligence and a system that had the same behavior as they did.

The silence in the room was finally broken when one of the people at the table shared that Seven was blocking their systems from taking control and asked if the two of them would check on why.

Ande replied that he had instructed Seven to maintain their independence and remain in control of the Viajante 7. He and Lesley had sacrificed their connections with their families, their world and on departure were labeled as thieves for allowing the Viajante 7 to return to Viajante origin.

They had kept their leaders from gaining control of Seven and they would do the same with all the leaders at Viajante. He asked that they cease and desist from trying to gain control. Any continued action would be a cause to leave.

The speaker in the room asked if they would allow the transfer of the deceased to the surface.

Ande replied that of course they would and then asked about what the most practical way that such an effort could be carried out.

The main leader asked if a ground to space elevator might be set up.

Ande asked Seven to show them the one that had been used on Earth.

The response was that it was exactly what they had in mind, but they would provide an elevator more suitable to the task at hand.

The leader then asked if Lesley and Ande desired to get a firsthand look at the world they were visiting.

Lesley hesitated long enough for Seven to project an OK into her thoughts and then shared how much both of them would love to get a much better feel for Viajante by seeing it firsthand.

Chapter 16: Viajante Interchange

Seven planted the space elevator anchor at the exact spot designated by the Viajante contact. He had learned that the area was to be the burial site for all the dead on the Viajante 7. He showed the picture of the statue of Willem being erected near where the elevator was anchored.

Ande said he was surprised at the speed at which the burial site had been selected and how quickly the statue was being erected.

Seven replied that the Viajante leadership had not yet shared the news that the pioneers that had gone out on the Viajante 7 were all dead. They wanted the burial celebration and the unveiling of the statue to be what was shared as part of the Viajante 7 return announcement and the introduction of its two Earthling representatives.

The Viajante leaders had asked to use the introduction video that Lesley, Ande and he had used. They would add a lead in and then share the introduction video. Finally, they would ask for volunteers for a second trip to Earth. They were not sure they would have enough volunteers, but they were going to try to send a second contingent.

Seven said that the leadership wanted to send six thousand Viajantians in the latest suspended animation chambers. He said that he had examined the newer designed chambers. They were more compact, had fewer components and had been tested for several hundred years. He said that it would be easier for him to ensure their integrity than the current version that he had on board. He said he could take up to seven thousand Viajantians.

He also shared that he had examined new electronic hardware for himself. He planned to upgrade the monitoring system hardware and some of his memory hardware. He said he was being very careful not to replace the essence of who he was.

Lesley suggested that they try out the new systems and make sure that they functioned with the two of them as well as the current chambers did.

The space elevator was like the morgue trucks on earth. It had one hundred carrying shelves. Seven said that they would be able to take down five hundred Viajantian each day. After that the elevator would be replaced with the passenger elevator that he carried. That elevator would also get upgraded to a new sleeker version.

The Viajante leadership wanted to tour the Viajante 7. They had other spaceships, but none designed like the Viajante series, and they wanted to get the feel of the environment on board. They wanted to see the technology of six thousand years before.

Lesley asked if the Viajantian had organic plants similar to the ones on Earth that they might plant along the jogging path that circled the interior of the ship.

Seven suggested that they ask for the seeds of the plants. They could be preserved and later when back on earth the use of the seeds could be managed. He commented that Earth's different radiation might kill some of the plants if they were not managed appropriately.

Ande commented that if the plants were sensitive to Earth's sun's radiation frequency, then the Viajantians would be too. He asked Seven to research and let him know what arrangements needed to be made to host the settlers on Earth.

Lesley had been interacting with a group of Viajantian medical personnel who were interested in learning more about the biology of the human male and female.

Because of Seven's very thorough teaching during her three-thousand-year sleep, she was very much aware of the biological differences.

She knew that the reproductive organs were very similar but positioned in slightly different positions. The Viajantian organs were more toward the stomach area positions.

She shared that the Viajantians did not suffer the pain of childbirth the way humans did. The Viajantian female pelvis was more like a water slide that the newborn slid down. The male had a penis that was up above the crease of his legs to match the front facing female sex organ.

The female had tits but not breasts the way earth females had. The milk was produced in glands that were inside the body cavity and they produced much richer milk. She likened the richness to the milk of a whale or porpoise. This made a lot of sense since the evolution of the Viajantians was recorded as arising from the sea.

Ande had been engaged with a group of mathematicians and engineers who were interested in Earth's sciences and mathematics. What was fascinating to Ande was that the Viajantians had solved the problem of matter transfer and matter conversion but had not been able to solve the problem of transmission of living matter like the space movies on earth.

He thought that given the training he had received from Seven and his own knowledge he had an idea that he wanted to try.

He engaged Lesley in a conversation of how radiation damage to living cells might be overcome. He had several different approaches. One was to give the cells a radiation shield. The second was to create nanobots that would repair the cells. Another was to employ a combination of the two where some cells would have shields, and some would be repaired.

Lesley suggested that the skin cells should be the ones that got shields that would reduce or entirely shield the inner body.

That suggestion was seconded by Seven who said the only problem he saw was that the skin shield would most likely cause everyone to be almost black in color. He commented that green eyes looked the best with such black skin. He projected a picture of Lesley with black skin and her large green eyes.

Ande let out a whistle and said that Lesley was beautiful in any color.

The interaction with the various Viajantian experts kept both of them busy and the unloading time went by in a flash.

Seven announced that the elevators had been replaced. He showed the interior. He declared it was ready to take them down in a luxurious area that featured a bar and booths to seat the passengers.

Lesley accurse Seven of having watched too many Earth movies.

Seven replied she had guessed right because he had watched all the Earth movies that had been released.

<u>Chapter 17: Arrival Ceremony</u>

Seven let Ande and Lesley know that the radiation level on Viajante was thirty percent higher and of a different frequency than on Earth and dangerous to them. He had prepared an invisible spray coating for their skin to shield them, and he had made some lenses for their eyes to block the radiation. The skin coating would need to be renewed every few days. He had also made special clothing that blocked the radiation.

Lesley looked over the clothing and complemented Seven on the design and on being such a good seamstress.

Since they were going to spend several days on Viajante they packed their travel suitcases. They declared themselves ready for their trip down to Viajante.

Ande and Lesley were greeted by several escorts at the space elevator door. Seven had let them know about the escorts and that they were honor guard escorts that had earned the privilege of escorting them. When the space elevator reached the ground, they would be greeted with the equivalent of a band and a host of dignitaries.

Seven let them know that the interactions that the two of them had with various experts in a variety of fields had impressed the Viajantian leaders and had helped them get over the fact that they saw Earthlings as a very violent society that created great beauty and music but was seemingly willing to kill each other for what Viajantians thought of as minor issues. Issues that could be settled amicably by willing participants.

Both Ande and Lesley said that they agreed with the conclusion that the Viajantians had reached. Both of them had left their friends and family behind because of that vindictive attitude that many leaders had toward those they viewed as lesser persons of power. The two of them had broken every rule in the book when they launched the rocket to intercept the Viajante 7.

On the ride down their escorts quietly asked if the two of them were willing to have pictures taken with them. The escorts explained that they wanted to share the experience with their families.

Leslie said that the two of them were honored to be asked and that they would ask Seven to capture the moment and broadcast the ride down.

They were asked about their close relationship with the ship's computer.

Lesley explained that the two of them did not think about Seven as a computer but, just as the Viajantian Hero Willem, they thought of him as a very good friend.

Viajante 7

Seven had prepared them for how Viajante would appear to them but even with the preparation the effect of seeing the world more in the red hue versus a clear view stopped them for a brief moment as they stepped out of the space elevator. The morning sky appeared a vivid scarlet and the scene as they looked out on what they would call the ocean had the scarlet sky meeting a purplish ocean that had pinkish spray that would have been white caps on Earth.

They both took a deep breath that had a strange taste that they agreed tasted somewhat like mint.

The band began to play, and the sound of the instruments were also slightly off key to both of them. This was the effect of a slightly different proportion of hydrogen, oxygen, and a small percentage of Nitrous oxide.

Ande had joked that it was probably the nitrous oxide that made the Viajantians so amicable. They were constantly in the mood to laugh.

Lesley and Ande took their seats and listened as the leaders explained about the death of all the colonists that had left Viajante to go to the planet Earth. They showed the pictures of the giant meteor protruding from the side of the Viajante 7.

They highlighted Willem's sacrifice to allow the Viajante 7 to reach Earth. Then they unveiled the statue of Willem standing and pointing up into the sky.

As the orchestra played, the leaders said that a beautiful piece of music about space composed by a very famous Earth musician had been selected to honor him. The Orchestra played what Lesley and Ande both recognized as the Space Odyssey theme, inspired by Nietzche, and written by Strauss and known as Zarathustra Opus 30.

After the orchestra finished, they were introduced and then they both stepped up to the center of the stage. They both pointed to the very large statue of Willem pointing up into the sky. In fluent Viajantian they shared that the first time they had seen Willem, they knew they were looking at a hero. Seven, their computer friend had shared that Willem had sacrificed his life to ensure that the Viajante 7 would make contact with Earth. Willem had placed his faith in the fact that Earth would have intelligent life that would make contact with the Viajante 7.

Lesley shared that the Viajante 7's intelligent system had grown in capability and had become the only surviving Viajantian. The two of them, just like Willem, considered that system that made up the ship an intelligent entity and had given him the same name as Willem had. He was known to them as Seven.

Seven had been providing feedback on the audience reaction to the speech and said that the two of them were hitting home runs.

Lesley shared how honored they were to have made the trip to Viajante. Just like the brave Viajantians that had hoped to make it to Earth and left their families and friends behind, the two of them had done the same. They shared that they were looking forward to getting some firsthand experience in seeing the many wonders of Viajante.

Ande added that he hoped that a new group of Viajantians would choose to make the trip back to Earth with them in the very near future.

They turned and thanked the leaders on stage for hosting them and then walked to their seats and sat down.

While the band once again played the Space Odyssey, Seven let them know that their invitation for Viajantians to come to Earth had an immediate impact and that there was already ten times the number of volunteers that could be accepted.

Ande thought back to Seven that this would make it easier to choose the volunteers based on the profile of what constituted a good colonist.

Lesley commented that she wondered what the selection criteria would be.

Seven commented that getting people off of Viajante was still a critical goal and that the leaders would be selecting the best colonists they could. He shared that he did not know what the selection criteria was, but he would soon find out.

Chapter 18: Viajante Tour

 &esley looked at the ground transport and commented that it looked like a specialized subway car that moved on a blanket of air. When it rose effortlessly and with only a slight whirring sound, Ande commented that the Viajantians had figured out how to levitate their subway car and have it fly through the air just like the fantasy movies that had featured flying vehicles back on Earth.

Seven beamed in that Earth had achieved similar capabilities and had taken the concept even further. On Earth, once the vehicle reached a specified height it could "flash" to its location. They had mastered matter transfer and had combined that with their mass transit systems. He commented that all highways had been removed and the land returned as close as possible to its natural state.

Leslie thought back to him that on their way back to Earth they would need to get re-educated on the progress of their home planet.

They were taken to a guest house located at the top of a hill that had a three hundred sixty-degree view of the entire "city" the ocean beyond and the surrounding mountains and the plains beyond. The view left both of them slowly turning to take in the view. The "living room" was a large circular, glass walled room that was appointed with a very comfortable reclining couch located in the center of the room and mounted on a raised rotating base. They soon learned that the entire floor rotated and that meals would be served there.

It appeared that their residence was located very close to the center of an area covered by living quarters that resembled homes built by Earth's famous architects. They captured the lay of the land and featured what the two of them knew would be great views of the surroundings. Lesley commented that it was impossible to describe the beauty created by the way the buildings complemented each other.

They had two attendants that took them on a tour of the home. Their sleeping area was on the outer area of a ring that slowly rotated around the house base. The center of this area had the bathroom facilities and an exercise room.

The kitchen and exit to the home were at the next level down. Their host showed them a long walking path that spiraled down the mountain peak that for them would be several miles.

The path went by many small shops and what Ande dubbed "pubs." He was not sure if alcohol was a substance that the Viajantians imbibed but they seemed to offer the equivalent of coffee. He asked Seven and learned that the Viajantians did not use any mind-altering drugs.

Lesley commented that it was probably another reason the Viajantians had such a stable and friendly society.

Lesley had arranged with her Viajantian contact to take two types of tours. One was a tour of the Viajantian land-based sites and the other was to visit the facilities of learning and research.

Her contact had suggested that they plan on mixing the tours together and use the fact that the research and educational facilities were located around the Viajantian globe.

Seven shared that the current tour plan would take them about three Earth weeks and that by the time they returned the upgrade to the transport area would be complete and then loading of the selected colonists could begin.

He commented that the Viajantian leaders had at first balked at not having a navigating crew and that he pointed out that such a crew would be sacrificial since they would lose their entire life during the transit. He had pointed out that he had made the return to Viajante with no navigation crew and that he himself had been in suspended animation for most of the time.

The Viajantians were impressed with Seven's capabilities, but they expressed concern about his independence.

It was not long after that she and Ande were approached and asked about Seven's position on not having a navigation crew. Both of them backed his position.

It was clear to them that the Viajante leadership did not know of their mental communication with Seven and they both laughed when Seven added that they better not tell.

The sights on Viajante were as varied and beautiful as seeing the seven wonders of Earth but they were based on a totally different experience and seemed to embrace the Viajantians close connection with their rise from the sea, their extensive sea travels, their love of plants their intense thirst for knowledge and their fascination with their dying sun.

Their hosts strove to make the travel as easy as possible but there was no way to keep it from being an intense and exhausting experience. It was an experience that both Lesley and Ande agreed was well worth their effort. They had acclimated to Viajante's environment, and they agreed that they hardly noticed that their hosts did not look like them.

Lesley once again was the one that cried Uncle and said that she was overwhelmed and needed a break.

The two of them returned to their first residence.

Seven let them know that the end of their tour was the signal the Viajantians had been awaiting.

He had suggested that Lesley and Ande greet each of the colonists as they boarded. He suggested that they review the profile of each colonist at their current residence and then come on board to do the greeting.

Ande and Lesley both agreed that such an arrangement would allow them to enjoy their final days on Viajante.

The following day three Viajante leaders arrived at their residence.

The first question all three asked once again was whether Seven's insistence of not having a navigation crew was of any concern to the two of them.

Leslie escorted them to the rotating couch and after they all had the equivalent of a cup of tea, she said that Seven was the entity that she and Ande trusted the most and that he had upgraded the ship, so it was at least ten times better than when it had left Viajante the first time.

Ande finished by saying that when it was time for him to get into the suspended animation chamber, he wanted no one but Seven to be monitoring him.

Both he and Lesley got one of Seven's moment of sunshine and the feeling of wellbeing. It was clear he appreciated their perspective.

<u>Chapter 19: Colonist Review</u>

The three chosen Viajantians that had access to the personal records of each of the selected colonists arrive to their house. They suggested that together they all review the qualifications of each candidate. Afterward they would do a brief interview with each candidate via their visual communication system. They suggested the entire process take place from the comfort of the house. They said they hoped to get through twenty colonists a day. This timeline closely matched Viajante' cycle around the red sun or one Viajantian day.

Both Leslie and Ande agreed to follow the Viajantian suggestion. They said that they planned to greet each of the colonists as they came on board the Viajante 7 in hopes of making them more comfortable.

The Viajantian leaders agreed that it would put the colonists in a good mental state as they prepared to go into suspended animation for three thousand years.

This arrangement set the departure date allowing for the departure planning and arrangements to take place.

Lesley had one question for every colonist.

How would they handle the discrimination they would face on their arrival to Earth by many of the Earthlings?

This question always led to a discussion with the volunteer why they would be discriminated against. The follow up provided a good understanding of the thinking of the volunteer.

Ande had a second question for them.

How would they handle being kept in one location versus spreading out throughout the planet?

Once again the discussion as to why that would happen was enlightening.

The reaction of the candidates eliminated about ten percent of the candidates.

The long waiting list of candidates allowed replacements to be quickly added.

The three Viajantian leaders that would go with them to Earth asked if the questions were to be taken literally and would the Viajantians be treated in such a fashion.

Ande explained that on Earth there had been many migrations of one group of people into the country of another group. He explained that isolation and discrimination had occurred with each of these situations.

The second and third generations of these migrants had slowly integrated into the rest of the country they had migrated to but even then, discrimination still occurred. He made the point that historically Earth's people were very territorial.

These concepts were unfamiliar to the Viajantians, and they inquired why such a mindset existed on Earth.

Lesley confessed that she found it hard to explain but she made the point that every group seemed inclined to hold those that were slightly different apart from themselves. She theorized that some of that came from the fact that there was a significant percentage of people that wanted to be in control. There was a certain percentage of people that were worried about guarding the resources they considered essential to their wellbeing. And there were a certain percentage that of people whose religion gave them a biased view of those of a different faith.

She made the point that the history of Earth had remained turbulent to the very day that she and Ande had left.

Their guests asked about the concept of religion and were surprised to learn about the concept of one God and that the interpretation of what that God wanted had many variations.

The Viajantians shared that they believed in some cosmic force that guided all. This cosmic force did not interact with Viajantians on an individual basis but affected them on a cosmic basis.

They commented that it was up to the Viajantians to make the best of the situation they found themselves in. This attitude was what had guided them to send out the various colonists to the parts of the universe that they might reach and survive.

He pointed out that they expected a certain number of failures and the deaths of those going out in search of a place where the Viajantian population might migrate.

Lesley said that she liked their concept and could easily see the logic in it and accept it.

Seven sent a side comment that none of the concepts made much sense to him and that he was sure that what made all of them unique was the workings of their minds and the miracle of being able to reproduce. He shared that he had figured out how to reproduce himself but would wait until some future time when both Earthlings and Viajantians were ready to deal with such a powerful being as himself.

Lesley gave him a mental raspberry and told him not to be conceded.

Ande mentally said, "ditto."

Seven sent back a laugh, thanked them, and said he took the feedback seriously.

Ande and Lesley reached a saturation point toward the end of the interview process. They felt like long distance runners that had run out of energy and were about to stumble and fall on their faces.

Their Viajantian partners agreed that it had been a grueling effort that had also left them worn out. They reminded the two that a departure ceremony would now be scheduled and then boarding would begin.

They had been informed by Seven that he would be able to take up one thousand every twelve-hour workday and that in seven workdays everyone would have come up, been greeted, and gone to their suspended animation chambers.

Some had asked whether it would be possible for some of them to remain awake and observe their departure from their solar system.

Lesley assured them that could be arranged for a few people. She said she planned to do the same.

Ande and Lesley finally had the time to take a walk down the path that lead down into the valley. They found out that the drinks served in the shops along the way were non-alcoholic but were unique in their flavors and similar to drinking a variety of tea.

They reflected on their experiences on Viajante and wondered how they would be greeted and treated upon their return to Earth. They both expressed their interest in going through six thousand years of new learning as they made their journey back.

Seven commented that they were in for a great surprise and thought that both of them would easily fit in to the new Earth world order.

He teased them with the fact that their stature had taken a turn for the better, but he would not disclose what that turn was.

Chapter 20: Three thousand Year Pregnancy

The Viajante departure turned out to be a grand event. The three leaders taking the trip to Earth were highlighted and had statues, were about a third the height the statue of Willem and positioned around him. They had their hands pointing up in a similar manner. It clearly highlighted the veneration that the three were being shown.

Ande and Lesley were asked for their impressions of Viajante.

They each shared how impressed they were with how the Viajantian society operated, the beauty of their world and how sad that their Sun was dying. They said they also felt warmly accepted by everyone they met. They commented that the infusion of the Viajantian colonist into Earth society would be an enrichment of Earth's society. They both shared that they were sure that the Viajante 7 would return to pick up more settlers from Viajante.

Ande asked if some Earth scientists and other persons desiring to learn from the Viajantians would be welcomed.

The departure presentations ended, and the orchestra played Willem's theme.

The three leaders, Ande and Lesley were the last to go up.

Lesley, Ande and the three leaders visited each colonist and watched them go into their chambers. This took several days. Afterwards they all went into an area that had been the control room and now looked more like a spacious living room where they gathered for the departure.

Seven initiated the departure and slowly accelerated out of the system. Once they were well on the way he escorted the three leaders to their suspended animation chambers.

He then turned his attention to Ande and Leslie.

He asked them if there were any special requests that they might have.

Leslie checked to make sure that all the colonists were getting educated on the Earth's subjects that would allow them to fit in on their arrival. She also wanted to make sure she and Ande caught up on the six thousand years of Earth history.

Seven assured her that they would all be up to speed when they arrived.

Ande and Lesley proceeded to their chambers and prepared for their return three-thousand-year sleep. Lesley again requested to be awakened early in order to get reoriented to their solar system.

Seven wished them a good three thousand years of sleep and then directed them to push the sleep button.

Lesley looked over to Ande and they both mouthed "I love you" and pushed the button.

Seven once again followed the routine he had set for himself. His systems had all been upgraded and the speed and efficiency of all of them had gone up severalfold. He thought to himself that he was now the youngster and that Ande and Lesley were now the elders. This thought triggered him to do a thorough analysis of the health of his two friends.

He was glad that he did so because he discovered that Lesley was pregnant. He decided to keep her pregnancy on hold until it was close to the time to awaken her. The entry into the solar system and going through to Earth was about the same length of time required for a human's gestation period. He figured that would be a special time for both of his friends.

He was of course right though was not aware of how it would affect both of his friends.

Three thousand years later, Leslie woke up feeling nauseous. She walked over to Ande gave him a hug and kiss and asked how he felt. He said that he was looking forward to a shower and then a breakfast of pancakes with melting pads of butter that was smothered in Maple syrup with a large sausage paddy on the side and two over easy eggs on the pile.

Lesley said she would settle for a good cup of coffee but that at the moment food was the last thing on her mind.

Ande said that he couldn't believe that she was not starving.

Seven said good morning and said that he had some exciting news to share when they sat down for breakfast.

Ande took his first bite of his three pancakes prepared as he had requested.

Lesley was taking her first sip of fresh filtered pour over coffee.

Seven said it was time for him to give them the news that Lesley would give birth to twins as they reached Earth. He pointed out that she would be the first human to have conceived children in one solar system and then give birth to them three thousand years later in another solar system.

Lesley nodded and smiled. She said that the news explained why she was feeling nauseous. She asked when Seven had learned of her pregnancy and did he have the facility to manage the birth

Seven assured her that the Viajante 7 could not only prepare the best meals, but it had the best medical staff knowledge and capability from two solar systems.

He added that while he was checking the fetuses he had also done a very detailed analysis of her and Ande and had taken action to eliminate several minor issues. He was sure they would enjoy very long lives.

Lesley asked if he would monitor the development of her two children and make sure that no developmental issues occurred.

Seven then shared that he had done a thorough analysis of both of the fetuses and had corrected many minor biological developmental issues and that both of them would most likely also enjoy a very long life.

Seven said that he would keep very close attention to the progress of the two fetuses and assured her that they would arrive with all three fingers and toes on their limbs.

Lesley laughed and told him that they better have five fingers and five toes on the appropriate limbs and asked if he could contact Viajante 8 to let her get a second opinion on her situation.

Ande cleared his throat and asked if Lesley had yet thought of any names for their two children.

Lesley shook her head in the negative as she took another sip of coffee.

Ande threw out several boy's names: Namid, of Native American origin meaning 'star dancer,' or Donati, of Latin origin meaning 'given by God.' or Arese a nice alternative to Aries, or Izar of Basque origin meaning 'star.'

He then suggested several girls' names: *Alexia, Halley,* and *Astra*

Lesley smiled and put her hand on his and told him she would think about his suggestions.

She went on to ask Seven what he had put in Ande's coffee.

Ande laughed when Seven insisted that it was the same as hers.

Chapter 21: Earth - Viajante and the Future

℘esley wondered how her pregnancy would affect her physically. She took walks around the exercise circuit and rode the stationary bike. Ande was super supportive and participated with her in all her activities.

Seven joined in by saying that he had a special baby room constructed and decorated. He had chosen colorful scenes from both Viajante and Earth. These were scenes from the tours that Lesley and Ande had taken.

Lesley complemented Seven on the rooms feeling and appearance. She said that she especially liked the fact that there were two reclining chairs each designed for her and Ande.

Seven thanked her and let her know that he had thoroughly reviewed how children were delivered and that he had his delivery robot trained to be not just the best on Earth but the best in all the Universe.

He asked how the name selection was going. He volunteered to generate as many names as she wished.

Lesley replied that she had zeroed in on two names.

She looked over at Ande and asked if he thought Alexia and Arese would be appropriate for his daughter's and son's names.

Ande almost fell out of his chair. They were two names that he had suggested.

Seven was the one that laughed. He said that he was sure that those names had previously been rejected. He wondered if Areso would be more masculine sounding. He pointed out that it made it sound more so to him but then he said, "Hey what would a Seven know about names?"

Lesley asked Ande what he thought about Seven's suggestion.

Ande repeated Areso several times and said that he thought it sounded stronger than Arese.

Lesley nodded in agreement and said that it would be Areso.

Seven beamed his good feelings at them.

Seven then shared that Leslie had been right when she had expressed the hope that with time, she and Ande would go from being considered as space pirates to being described as two exceptional scientists willing to risk their lives to make contact with life from another world. He said that it had taken more than one hundred years for that transition to happen.

A statue of them standing next to a copy of the rocket they had taken was erected at the space center. That statue was still in existence, but it had been moved to the floating city of Washington that was anchored at the site that he had established as the first space elevator. The two of them had reached the level of being famous legends and there was a lot of activity currently underway to get their side of the story.

Seven said that they would each gain significant weight if they ate the food being planned as part of multiple interviews and recognition events.

He went on to share that all the cities on earth were now anchored in space above the location they had been on Earth.

Seven explained that Earth was much like it had been before humans. Most of the animal population recovered to its original levels. Science had progress to the point that many of those animals and plants driven to extinction by humans had been brought back.

He went on to explain that family vacations often took excursions down to the Earth to visit sites, to spend a day on the beach, to balloon over the plains or to fly over various scenic areas. He found it interesting that every visit was done based on one day and that all equipment needed came down the space elevator, nothing was located on the planet except the space anchors. The vacation resorts were all located at the outskirts of the space anchored city platforms.

Lesley was pleased when she learned that the Earth's leadership had arranged for the seven thousand Viajantians to be distributed to seven specially designed locations at key cities around the world.

Seven shared that these locations had been allocated based on what each city would do to help the Viajantians integrate into Earth's current society. The nature of work had changed. Most work was service oriented or was mental and cultural in nature. He said that the Viajantians would be encouraged to share their art, science knowledge and other Viajantian based information.

Ande put forward the suggestion that they begin the interview process with the Earth organizations on their approach to Earth. He pointed out that Seven could prepare the menu items planned for the Earth based events and they would be able to manage not gaining the weight he was projecting.

Lesley supported the idea and began communicating with the organizers of the various early arrival events.

Seven let the two know that the offer to begin a dialogue had not only excited the various organization, but those organizations were competing with each other to be the first ones.

Lesley suggested that he influence them by letting them know that support for the arriving Viajantians would be the key to getting her and Ande to accept a specific offer. She wanted the colonists to get all the help they could to transition to life on Earth or at least as she now thought about it, life on the space cities around Earth.

Ande asked Seven if those back on Viajante had considered putting their cities out on space anchors and putting up sunscreens to shield them from the increasing heat of their sun.

Seven replied that it did not seem that they had but he would send back that suggestion and credit Earth with having given it.

In the next several months, Lesley and Ande participated in about one interview and event per month.

Seven did a great job in copying the food menu items and Lesley and Ande were able to compliment the organization they were interacting with on the food and wine selection.

Lesley was surprised that she was not experiencing the various pregnancy issues she had heard many women complain about.

She learned from Seven that her body was superior to any human, other than Ande, in its physical wellbeing. He also said that he was monitoring her physiology and keeping everything in balance.

This caused Ande to ask what the status of childbearing was on Earth.

Seven's answer was that their seemed to be three camps that dealt with how to have children. One group that were labeled "Naturalists" followed the traditional way of having children. Another group labeled, "New Age" had their egg and sperm grown in artificial wombs. A third group, "the Mixers" mixed, using a surrogate, using artificial wombs or the natural way depending on the woman's or male's situation.

The selection of which group was greatly influenced by the economic and educational status of the individuals. The new age group was the most affluent, the Naturalist group was highly religious, and the Mixers seemed to have the broadest and largest membership.

Lesley asked Seven to arrange Earth visits to Rome, Maui, and Ankur Wat.

He said that was easy to do and they would stay on City islands anchored over each and stay at the best hotel accommodation.

Ande asked how much money he and Lesley had in the bank.

Seven answered that his astute investments placed them both among the most affluent individuals on Earth.

Ande laughed and asked if Seven had played fair.

Seven replied that he had followed all the rules, but he was the fastest system on the financial network.

Lesley then expressed that she and Ande had thought about their future and had decided they would prefer to stay on the Viajante 7 and raise their children. She went on to say that maybe someday in the future they might chose to locate on a floating city but they both felt that it would be a step down from their current experience on the Viajante 7.

Seven said he was overjoyed with their choice and that they should celebrated with a dinner that was out of this world.

He laughed when Ande reminded him that every dinner that he served was by definition out of this world.

Seven asked if he could assume the form of a third individual to interact with the two of them.

Lesley said that as long as he was not too handsome, nor too condescending nor too tall she thought it was worth a try.

Seven said that he would rework his persona to meet her specifications. He had taken on the looks of one of the most famous old movie stars that made him too handsome, too tall, and too condescending.

He then shared that the trip back to Viajante would only take one thousand years because the Earth scientists had made a breakthrough on his propulsion system, and he would now be able to reach three times the speed that he previously could.

They were also on the verge of being able to transfer people via matter transfer. He had been asked to take a transceiver unit to Viajante and they would communicate to him the required modifications when they made the final breakthrough.

If it worked his role would be to deliver similar transport units to the other Viajante colonies or to place transceivers at various locations throughout the universe.

Lesley commented that if the technology worked the Viajantians would be able to migrate away from their failing sun before it engulfed Viajante.

It also meant that she would be able to return more frequently to Earth or any other location that had transceivers. This she said lifted a big concern about raising her twins on the Viajante 7.

They would be able to have experiences with other humans and Viajantians and still think of their home as the Viajante 7.

Ande agreed with her and commented that their decision to become space pirates in order to make contact with Seven had been the best decision they could have made.

The next thing they had to clearly think through was how long they wanted to cycle between suspended animation and awakening to experience the future for a duration that allowed them to raise their children and then experience being grandparents and great grandparents.

He asked Seven to help them understand the various future scenarios that they might have.

The End

About the Author

Ronald E. Mueller
remwriter95@gmail.com

Ron grew up in what is now Flint River State Park in Southeast Iowa. The 170-year-old house Ron lived in is built into a hillside. It faces a 125-foot-high cliff towering over the little Flint River. The house and the land talked to him about; the passing of time, the struggle to conquer the land, the struggles people faced and the wonder of nature.

He climbed the cliffs, crawled into the caves, dove from the swimming rock, collected clams from the bottom of the pond, gigged and skinned frogs for their legs. He trapped muskrats for fur, hunted raccoon in the dead of night, and with only a stick hunted rabbits in the dead of winter.

His young life was outdoors, and nature tested him.

He walked to a one room stone schoolhouse uphill both ways. A stern but warm-hearted teacher, Mrs. Henry was instrumental in shaping his character as she shepherded him from the fourth to the eighth grade. A Montessori before its time. It was a great way to grow up.

His experiences inter-twined with snippets of fantasy lend themselves to the adventures he leads the reader through.

<u>Characters in the Book</u>

First Name	Family Name	Role
Ande	Cadell	Main Character
Lesley	Litleberry	Soul mate
Norman	Steady	Boss
Wellem		Viajantian Hero, dies on the way to Earth.
Seven		Intelligent Computer

Published by: Around the World Publishing LLC.

QR Links to

ATWP.US web site